THE SHIFTING FATE SERIES

BOND OF
DESTINY

THE SHIFTING FATE SERIES

BOND OF DESTINY

TESSA HALE

Copyright © 2021 by Tessa Hale. All rights reserved.

No part of this book may be reproduced in any form or by any electronic or mechanical means, including information storage and retrieval systems, without written permission from the author, except for the use of brief quotations in a book review.

This is a work of fiction. Names, characters, places, and incidents are either the products of the author's imagination or are used fictitiously. Any resemblance to actual persons, living or dead, businesses, companies, events, or locales is entirely coincidental.

Cover Design: MIBL Art
Paperback Formatting: Champagne Book Design

CHAPTER ONE

ALL I COULD THINK WAS THAT IT FELT LIKE COTTON balls had been shoved down my throat. My tongue stuck to the roof of my mouth and my lips were painfully dry. I rolled to my side and the darkness around me swirled and pitched.

I blinked. Fluorescent light pierced the darkness. Images came in snapshots. Stained cement floor. Dingy cot. Metal bars.

It was the bars that had me jerking upright. It was a bad move. Everything around me swam in a mix of color and light. A wave of nausea swept through me.

"Try not to move too quickly. The drugs can really throw you for a loop."

I swung around towards the female voice, which only brought on more nausea. I closed my eyes for a moment, giving my stomach a chance to settle.

"Breathe in through your nose and out through your mouth. It helps."

I did as the voice instructed. After a dozen or so breaths, I felt better. The nausea wasn't gone, but I was no longer in danger of tossing my cookies. I cracked my eyes open. I came face-to-face with a girl about my age, sitting cross-legged on a cot in the cell next to mine.

"Hi," I croaked.

The girl gave me a shaky smile. "Hi. I'm Rezah."

"Rowan." I quickly scanned the other six cells. It was clear we were in a basement of some sort. There were cinder block walls and no windows. "Where are we?"

Any hint of warmth fled Rezah's expression. She hugged her knees to her chest. "I don't know."

"Who took us?" I searched my mind for the last thing I remembered. Jaz. The Diet Coke. When I got out of here, I was going to kill her.

"We can't talk about them," Rezah whispered.

Them. A group. A pack. Who? I opened my mouth to press the girl but saw she was trembling, her eyes darting around as if someone might jump out and attack her at any moment. I needed another tack. "Where are you from?"

Rezah focused back on me. "The Lakeland pack in Michigan."

My eyes widened a fraction. "Is that where we are? Michigan?" With no windows, I couldn't tell if the landscape around was at all familiar. For all I knew, we could've been in Dubai.

"I don't know," she said softly.

"How long have you been here?"

Rezah's dark hair was long and a little bit scraggly. Something that spoke of going without brushing or a haircut for too long. She looked at the cinder block wall. That

2

was when I saw it. Tally marks carved into the rock. Her eyes roamed over the grooves. "A little over nine months."

My stomach gave a vicious cramp. Nine months. I'd never make it that long. A pang lit in my chest, claws digging deep. My bond. My mates. Tears stung my eyes as I rubbed my sternum. They had to be going crazy by now. I opened my mind to the pack link, reaching out. There was only silence.

"Our mind links don't work here."

My gaze snapped to Rezah. "That's not possible."

"He has powerful shields working for him. You can't use your gift. You can't reach out to your family. You can't even shift because they drug you every day." A tear slid down Rezah's cheek, but she didn't lift a hand to wipe it away. As if she'd gotten so used to them falling, she didn't even notice anymore.

"Who?" I pushed.

Rezah started shaking again. This time worse than before. "Don't say his name."

Something scratched at the back of my mind. A memory. An SUV. That familiar voice calling me *daughter*. Ice slid through my veins. My birth father. That was who had us. And I knew him. But I couldn't get my mind to quite make the leap.

Rezah hugged her knees tighter to her chest and began to rock back and forth. I felt like the worst kind of monster. "It's okay. You don't have to tell me."

What I needed to focus on now was getting out of here. I closed my eyes and felt for my wolf. She was there, somewhere deep in that golden pool of energy, but when I tried to bring her forth, I couldn't. I tugged harder, trying to bring the energy around me. Nothing.

I let out a frustrated breath, sweat breaking out on my brow. I closed my eyes again, searching for my connection to the guys. I could still feel them, pinpricks of light on the darkest night, but they felt a million miles away. Forming a message with my mind, I pushed it out into the darkness.

It was almost as if the words echoed back at me from stone walls. Nothing could get through. Panic lit deep in my belly, but I focused on keeping my breathing even.

I opened my eyes and pushed off the cot. My legs were shaky, either from the drugs or from going too long without food. I moved first to the door of the cell, studying the lock. It was key-coded. If I could fry the lock mechanism or even the bars themselves, I bet I could break free.

Feeling for that golden pool of energy again, I focused on my anger. My rage. Jaz. Whoever had taken me. Being separated from my mates.

I let all of the emotion fuel me, then shot out a hand. There was a buzzing sensation, but nothing happened. I could feel the start of my gift taking hold, but then it simply fizzled out.

Hell. I searched the walls for any point of weakness. There was a curtained area at the back of the cell. I moved towards it and pulled the fabric back. There was a bathroom that looked like it belonged in a prison. A toilet with no lid. The tiniest sink I'd ever seen. And a shower about a foot and a half wide.

My stomach twisted. This place was designed for extended stays. *Nine months.* Rezah's words echoed in my head.

Panic raced through me, but I shoved it down and stepped back into the cell. I closed my eyes again, trying to open my mind. Luc had said he could always sense me as long as I opened myself to him.

"What are you doing?" Rezah asked.

"Trying to contact my mates. If I can just clear my mind, my empath will sense me."

She was silent for a moment as I focused. "They can't find you, Rowan. No one can."

CHAPTER TWO

SOMETHING ABOUT THE BLEAKNESS IN REZAH'S VOICE had my hands curling into fists. My fingernails dug into my palms, but I welcomed the bite of pain. It kept me grounded.

"Do you have mates?"

She nodded, more tears coming. "Three. But the bond was only cemented with one."

"How are you alive?" The question just poured out of me. Only one day without my mates before had almost finished me. I didn't understand how Rezah was still breathing.

She leaned against the wall, staring off into space. "More drugs. They found something that keeps you alive."

"And your mates?" I was almost too scared to ask.

"They're okay. I can still *feel* them and I think they can feel me too. It's only if we die that they're in danger." Rezah's gaze turned to me. "We have to fight for them."

"I'll never stop fighting for them. These assholes won't win."

Her mouth curved in a sad smile. "They'll do anything they

can to break you. Anything they can to get you to relinquish your bond."

I stiffened. "I thought it was possible to force the breaking of a bond."

"It is, but some of your power is lost in that breaking. If you choose to break it, none is lost. *He* doesn't want to lose a morsel of our gifts. Not when he could use them." Rezah spat the words, her hatred bleeding through each one.

A new wave of nausea swept through me. I'd never sever my tie to my bond. I'd hold on with everything I had in me. No matter what.

I started to ask Rezah another question when the creaking of metal sounded.

"Step away from the bars," Rezah hissed. "The guards don't like it if you seem too interested in your cage."

The use of the word *cage* had my wolf pawing at my insides. I did my best to soothe her, promising vengeance to whoever had put us here, but it only did so much. I moved until my back was pressed against the cold, stone wall.

Footsteps echoed on the cement floor. A girl with red hair and freckles appeared. She would've been beautiful if it wasn't for the dead look in her eyes. It was as if there was a haze over them. She saw what was in front of her but didn't completely take it in.

The girl carried what looked to be two trays. She bent, sliding one under an opening in Rezah's cell. "You need to eat everything." Even the girl's voice was robotic.

Rezah glared at the girl. "Would you want to eat this garbage, Angie?"

She straightened. "We should be grateful for everything that's provided for us. If you would like another meal, you know what you have to do."

"And what's that?" I asked, pushing off the wall. There was nothing about this petite girl that was frightening in any way.

She slid the cardboard tray into my cell. "Sever your bonds. Pledge your loyalty to the true Alpha King."

The true Alpha King? That sounded like some crazy, cult rhetoric. No, thank you. "And if I don't want to?"

Angie shrugged. "You'll stay here until you see things differently. Or you'll die."

She said it so casually. As if dying was akin to losing a hair tie.

"Eat everything. You'll need your strength."

"For what?" I pressed.

A hint of something passed over Angie's eyes. Fear maybe? "You'll need to be shown the error of your ways. You'll see. There's a better way. All I had to do was let go."

My hands fisted more tightly, my nails digging into my palms. She had stood where I was now. And she was putting others through the same torture she had experienced. "How can you look at yourself in the mirror?"

Angie didn't flinch, but those unfocused eyes came to me. "He knows what's best. How to make us the strongest we can be."

"*He* took away your free will."

"Don't bother," Rezah muttered. "Angie has fully drunk the Kool-Aid."

I moved to the bars, wrapping my hands around the metal. "You can let us out of here. Give us a chance."

Something else flickered across Angie's expression, but then she closed down again. "He knows best. You'll see."

I whirled to Rezah. "He knows best? What is this creepy shit she keeps muttering?"

Rezah shivered. "They try to break you. Your mind as much as your body."

My stomach revolted, the threat of what might be to come combined with a drug hangover and the smell of greasy steak swirling together. I'd already been through hell this past year. People had come for me time and again. I wasn't going down without a fight.

Rezah nodded at me, her shoulders rolling back. "Keep hold of that fire. You'll need it."

"It won't help," Angie said. "You'll break eventually. You're just making it more painful for yourself this way."

Rezah leapt from her cot and charged at the bars. "Just because you gave up on your mates doesn't mean we will. I won't sign their death warrants the way you did."

Angie blanched and her eyes took on an even more faraway look. For the first time, I felt real pity for the girl. Her trauma had sent her so deep inside herself, the girl she had been no longer existed.

"It's okay," I told Rezah quietly. "We'll help each other hold on." We could remind each other what we were fighting for.

Footsteps echoed on the cement. "Now, girls. What are all the raised voices about?"

Rezah scampered back from the bars, her whole body trembling. But I couldn't move. Because I'd come to know that voice over the past month. Ever since the Quad had first arrived.

The man stepped into view, a grin twisting his lips. "Hello, daughter."

CHAPTER THREE

KALEB. MY MIND FLASHED TO HIS MOMENTS OF kindness. Offering me and my bond refuge. Cutting himself so that one of my pack wouldn't be harmed. His support of me staying at Ridgewood.

Now I saw all of those moments through a different lens. A harsher one.

"Why?" It was the only thing I could seem to get out.

He moved closer to the cell and Angie took an immediate step back, her eyes cast downward. Kaleb barely seemed to notice her. "There are forces at play here that you don't know about."

"Then explain it to me," I gritted out.

His mouth curved, amusement lining his expression. "I do like your spunk. Even in the situation you find yourself in now, you still have that hint of fire."

"You mean the situation *you* put me in."

"You were the one good thing your mother gave me. She turned out to be a disappointment in so many other ways."

My muscles locked, a burning anger lighting deep inside. "What do you want from me?"

Kaleb picked an invisible piece of lint off his shirt. "Did you know the shifter world once had a ruling court?"

"I didn't ask for a history lesson. I asked what you want from me."

His eyes flashed, the first real hint of temper. "Listen when I'm talking, Rowan."

I bit the inside of my cheek, tasting blood.

"That's better. We used to be governed by a king. He was served by a court. We were powerful then. Gifts were plentiful and strong. As we've tried to divide up leadership, give more people a voice, those powers have waned. That's not a coincidence."

As far as I'd learned, the vast majority of shifters in our world had very little voice. Even Mason, the leader of our pack, had little to no sway over the Quad and the laws and rules they made. There had simply been a different name put on that ruling court.

Kaleb studied me through the bars. "It's time to return to our old ways. Time to elevate those of us with powers to those positions."

"And let me guess, you're just meant to be king?" I couldn't help the sarcasm that slipped into my voice.

Kaleb's eyes flashed. "Watch your tone. You have a choice here. You have a chance to rule alongside me. To have a bond truly worthy of your power. I have chosen wolves who will turn you into the ultimate weapon. No one will stand in our way."

My throat tightened as my mouth went dry. A tool to hurt people. That was all he wanted me for. To use me until I had nothing left. Then he would cast me aside like so many others had.

The only people who hadn't were my bond. Lucas. Keene. Anson. Vaughn. Holden. My heart ached as I held their names in my mind. "I will never betray my bond. Never."

A look of disappointment filled Kaleb's expression. "I was afraid you'd say that. You'll come to see things my way. It just may take a little *convincing*." He turned towards the hallway. "Garrison."

More footsteps echoed in the room and Rezah let out a faint whimper. A hulking man appeared, and I swore the floor shook with each of his steps. Garrison came to a stop in front of Kaleb.

"I'm afraid my daughter isn't seeing things our way just yet. You may proceed with your first session."

A grin spread across Garrison's face. It was nothing short of gleeful. "Level authorization?"

"She is my daughter. Let's keep it at a five for now. I'd like a full report when you're finished."

"Of course, Alpha." Garrison pulled a sort of baton from his tactical pants.

Angie let out a small, strangled sound and hurried down the hall and disappeared.

I stared straight ahead. I wouldn't let them see me cower. Wouldn't give them the gift of my fear. I met my father's gaze. "You show your weakness by trying to force your will on others."

A muscle in his cheek fluttered. "I'm showing my dominance."

"If it were true dominance, you'd fight me one-on-one. You wouldn't try to dull my powers and strip me of everything fate has given me." I had no idea how things would turn out if Kaleb and I went head-to-head, but I knew I'd have a better chance at surviving that than staying in this dungeon.

Kaleb tipped his head back and laughed. "Oh, Rowan. This is a kindness I'm showing you. If you and I fought, I'd rip you apart."

"Prove it."

His mouth pressed together in a thin line. "Killing you would be such a waste. You have so much to give to our cause. You simply don't know it yet."

It would never happen. Never. I'd find a way out. Even if it took years.

Kaleb's lips twitched. "That fire will be fun to break and remold. I can't wait to see it pointed at an appropriate adversary."

"I think I'm seeing one right now."

He chuckled. "I have a feeling you'll be singing a different tune rather soon. Remember, your gifts don't work down here. My shields have imbued the walls and bars with their gifts. But you still have your shifter healing. We'll break you again and again. As many times as it takes."

Kaleb turned to Garrison, the amusement falling from his expression. "I'm counting on you."

"I won't let you down, Alpha."

Kaleb gave him a curt nod, turned on his heel, and left.

A feral smile stretched across Garrison's face. "I like the fiery ones. The ones that cower shatter too easily."

He punched a code into the door, and it swung open. I stood my ground. I kept my stance loose, my weight on the balls of my feet. I played Anson's self-defense lessons over and over in my mind.

Garrison tapped the baton on his open palm. I watched his weight shift back and forth. My one advantage would be speed. Garrison was a lumbering giant. I was a quarter of his size and could hopefully avoid the majority of his blows.

The cell door clanged behind him. "Changed your mind yet?"

"No," I gritted out.

"Bad choice." He swung the baton out, and I dodged the

worst of the hit. I gave a quick hook shot to his kidney, but it felt like hitting a brick wall.

Garrison grunted and turned with more speed than I thought him capable of. The baton hit me with so much force, it stole the air from my lungs. Then a white-hot pain lit along my ribs. At least one had to be broken.

I wheezed against the fire in my side and skidded out of the path of a second blow. When I avoided the third, Garrison let out a growl. He looked down at his baton and flipped some sort of switch. Electricity crackled.

Garrison chuckled at the sparks. "Your little energy gift doesn't work anymore."

I didn't have a chance to question what that would mean for me before a bolt of electricity shot out, landing in my middle. My muscles seized and I crumpled to the floor. Fire lit through me, and my mouth opened in a silent scream.

CHAPTER FOUR

A COOL RAG GHOSTED OVER MY FOREHEAD AS MY BODY shook with painful tremors. Ones that felt like they rattled my bones.

"What's wrong with her?" a deep voice asked.

"I don't think the medication is able to stabilize her. She needs her bond."

Some part of me recognized Rezah's voice through the sea of pain. Whether the pain was from a week of repeated beatings or the fact that I was dying, I couldn't tell. Whatever drug they were giving me to keep me tethered to this world without my bond wasn't working.

The guard chuckled. "Nice try. That's not happening."

Another especially vicious tremor rocked me. Hands tugged a thin covering up around my shoulders.

"Can you at least get me another blanket? I don't think the *Alpha King* is going to be too happy if his daughter dies on your watch."

The guard muttered a curse. Footsteps echoed in retreat.

"Rowan, can you open your eyes?" The cloth moved over my forehead again.

I tried to do as she asked, to force my lids to rise, but they felt so incredibly heavy. One finally cracked open. The fluorescent light felt like burning acid on my eyes.

Rezah moved, blocking out the worst of it. "Here. Take a sip of this. You need to stay hydrated." She tipped a paper cup to my lips, and I slowly lifted my head to drink.

I'd realized over the past week that they never gave us anything with any heft. Disposable plates and cutlery. Nothing that could ever be used as a weapon.

The water had a rusty aftertaste to it, but it felt like heaven on my throat. My head fell back to my cot. The worst of my injuries from my most recent session with Garrison had healed, but everything hurt. The world around me swam, as darkness teased the corners of my vision.

"Stay with me," Rezah ordered, squeezing my arm. "Don't pass out."

But it was too late. The darkness was taking me under.

———⋇———

"Fix her!"

Kaleb's bellow grated on my ears. Sound and light pricked at me, but I could barely reach them. I was drowning in a sea of darkness.

Rowan.

It sounded like Lucas. Too much like him.

Tears burned my eyes. I so badly wanted it to be him. Wanted to feel that warmth that was only Luc.

Ro, can you hear me?

Cold fingers pressed against my neck. The touch hurt. As if it were made of barbed wire.

My eyes fluttered open. "Rowan, look at me."

Slowly my focus solidified on a woman in front of me. "Tell me what you feel."

"Hurts."

It was the only word I could get out. My chest felt like it was being shredded from the inside out. I was burning up, yet freezing. Electrical shocks shot through me.

Kaleb's face filled my vision. "Sever the bond now, before it's too late."

"No," I croaked.

"Damn it, Rowan. Do it now!"

I pressed my lips together into a hard line. I wouldn't. I'd take death before I let my mates go. A tear slipped free, sliding down my face and onto the cot.

Kaleb whirled on the woman. "Why isn't your drug working?"

The woman's hands trembled slightly. "I don't know. It's possible her bond is too strong. We've never used the medication on a bond of six, especially not one with a gift as strong as hers."

"How are you going to fix it?" he growled.

"I don't know yet. I need to run some tests. But she may not make it that long. You may need to release her back to her mates—"

The woman's words were cut off as Kaleb struck out, grabbing her by the neck. "You should've been prepared for this."

"I'm sorry, Alpha." Her words were barely audible as Kaleb's fingers tightened, cutting off her air supply.

"Not good enough." With one swift movement, he snapped her neck.

17

I couldn't hold in my whimper as Kaleb dropped her to the floor. His gaze shot to the two guards in the corner of the cell. "One of you, clean up this mess. The other, get Rebecca's assistant and see if he can fix her fuckup."

"Yes, Alpha."

Kaleb turned to Rezah, who was pressed against the wall. "Take care of her. If she dies, you die too."

My body shook, each tremble sending sparks of pain throughout my system. It was too much, an overload of agony. The darkness closed in again.

———⟨✕⟩———

Rowan. Where are you? I can feel you. Talk to me.

It was Luc again. Only it wasn't. I knew it was impossible. Only a fevered creation of my mind.

I want it to be you. I sent the words back into the nothingness of my imagination.

Ro! It is me.

It's not. I know it's not. You can't be real.

A growl echoed in my mind. *It's me. I learned to break through some elements of shielding. Listen to me.*

I wanted to believe him so badly, but I was so tired. Everything was so heavy. I only wanted to slip away.

Ro. Stay with me. Don't leave me. Please.

There was such desperation in his tone, it forced me to hold on. *Love you, Luc.*

I love you too. We're going to fix this. Who has you?

Kaleb.

The sound of curses filled my mind.

I struggled to get out the next thoughts. Even without speaking them out loud, they hurt too much. *He's my father.*

There was silence for a moment. *I'm so sorry, Ro. We're coming to get you. You just have to tell us where.*

I don't know. A basement jail. I'm so tired.

Just hang on. We need to complete the bond.

It was my fault we hadn't. I'd held back from Holden because he'd hurt me. I hadn't been ready to place my heart in his hands again, too scared he might break it. But it was too late. I couldn't reach him. *Tell Holden I'm sorry.*

Tell him your damn self, Luc gritted out.

Ro?

My throat tightened at the sound of Holden's voice in my head. Even through my unconsciousness, I could feel the tears sliding down my cheeks. There was no way this was real, but I wanted it so badly.

Holden. His name was a prayer on my lips. A reckless hope for an impossibility.

Feel me.

Holden's words were a gentle command I had no choice but to obey. I let myself be pulled towards the sound of him. Towards that faint spark of light. I swore his heat wrapped around me.

Ro, I love you. You have me, always. Let yourself fall.

In that moment, a million memories swirled around me. Holden's care and protectiveness. His grin and deep blue eyes. The way he tried to care for everyone around him. It didn't matter that our journey hadn't been perfect. I loved him with everything I had.

I could feel the tethers keeping me from Holden. The ties that had kept me from cementing the last of our bond. In a single breath, I released them. Then I was falling. But a pool of light caught me. It was warmth and comfort. It was the feeling of balanced wholeness.

Pain flared on my hip, and I gasped as my eyes flew open.

Rezah's face filled my vision. "Oh God, Rowan. I thought you weren't going to wake up. How are you feeling?"

I couldn't think about her words or question. My mind was only filled with one thing. A certainty to the depths of my bones. "They're coming."

CHAPTER FIVE

I PULLED THE WAISTBAND OF MY SWEATPANTS DOWN, lifting my T-shirt slightly. Rezah gasped. The entirety of my mark was filled in. Each point on the star and the center that signified me.

"How?" she whispered.

"I don't know. I felt Luc in my head. I thought it was just the fever, but he said he'd broken through the shields around me. He connected me with Holden and…" My voice trailed off as tears stung my eyes. My bond was complete. Already the worst of the tremors and fever had subsided. But I felt like I'd fought a battle. In many ways, I had.

"I've never heard of something like this happening. A bond cementing when the two individuals aren't together." Rezah's eyes widened as she took me in. "They have no idea just how powerful you are."

I gripped her hand. "Don't tell them."

"I won't say a word. We need to make them believe the medication had a delayed effect. But you can't let them see your mark."

I quickly tucked my T-shirt into the band of my sweats and

tried reaching out with my mind. *Luc?* My voice echoed in my mind. But it wasn't the same echo as when I'd first arrived here. It was as if I stood at the end of a long tunnel.

His voice echoed back. *Keene thinks he found you. We're coming.*

The words were faint, and I could hear the strain in them. Luc was pushing himself to the breaking point to reach me.

Be safe. Love you.

Love you, Ro.

Then he was gone. Panic lit in me at the loss of Luc. My tie to my bond. I breathed through it, pressing my hand to my mark. I carried all of them with me now. They were a part of me. The me that was stronger than I ever could've imagined.

"You're talking to them, weren't you?"

I looked up at the sound of Rezah's voice. There was such longing in it. I spoke so softly I could barely make out my own words. "They said they think they've found where we are."

Her fingers dug into my hands. "They're coming?"

I nodded. "We need to be ready."

Swinging my legs over the side of the cot, I tried to stand. I immediately sat back down. My muscles couldn't keep me upright, but I didn't let the panic get hold of me again. I would find a way to fight. "Did they leave us any food?"

Rezah stood and crossed to the corner of the cell. "They left crackers and juice for you since you were throwing up earlier."

I twisted off the cap of the juice and chugged it. The orange flavor was too sweet on my tongue after days of nothing, but I had to hope the sugar in it would help. Rezah tore open the package of crackers and handed it to me. I shoved one after another into my mouth, barely chewing before swallowing.

"Careful. You don't want to get sick."

I forced myself to slow down with the next cracker, to chew more thoroughly. Only after the entire sleeve was gone did I stop.

Rezah surveyed my face. "Your color's better."

"The worst of the pain's gone. I just feel weak."

She worried her bottom lip. "I hope they bring plenty of backup. There are at least twenty guards."

"You counted?"

"I've tried to memorize the switching of the shifts, who to expect when. I listen when they talk on their earpieces."

I reached out and gripped Rezah's hand. "We're getting out of here. We're going home."

Her eyes glistened. "I can't even remember what home looks like. I wonder if I just made things up in my head. Was my porch swing as comfortable as I imagine? Was my house gray or blue?"

My heart ached for Rezah, but hearing her fears fueled the anger deep inside me. I gripped it tightly. I needed every last bit of energy it could give me. I stoked it with the memories of every blow, every taunt Garrison had leveled on me. I'd keep the fire fed with the pain etched into my bones.

"We're going to make them pay."

Rezah's eyes flared. "Garrison is mine."

She had lived with the enforcer's torture for eons longer than I had. I could give her that. Rezah's gaze traveled over the cell. "I wish we could shift."

"Me too." My wolf pawed at my chest, longing to get free. I couldn't imagine how badly Rezah wanted to be one with her other half. I sent a silent promise to my wolf that soon she'd get her wish.

The telltale sound of the metal door echoed in the quiet

space, followed by footsteps. There were too many to belong to only one person. A second later, Kaleb appeared with a group behind him. Garrison, two other guards, and an older man I didn't recognize.

Kaleb's steps faltered as he saw me sitting up. "Is she better?"

The question was directed at Rezah not me. She nodded woodenly. "The medication must've had a delayed reaction with her. She woke up an hour ago. Her fever has broken and she's no longer shaking."

He turned to me, gaze assessing. "How do you feel?"

"Weak but better." I needed him to see me as no threat to him.

Kaleb glanced at the man I didn't recognize. "It looks as if your services are no longer needed."

"Are you sure that's such a good idea?" Garrison asked. "We should break her bond and be done with it. It's too much of a risk."

My entire body locked. Break my bond. The words swirled in my mind.

"You question me?" Kaleb demanded.

Garrison immediately lowered his eyes. "Of course not. I just want to make sure her power doesn't go to waste. You've waited so long."

"I'll expect to be paid either way," the stranger said. "The contract has already been signed."

Kaleb's jaw went hard. "I won't waste a drop of her power."

The man shrugged. "Your choice. But she's already regaining strength. I can feel it from here. If she overtakes you, I won't be able to help."

Wariness filled Kaleb's expression as he glanced in my

direction. "Fine, break it. But save as much of her strength as possible."

"Of course," the man said with a dip of his head.

I leapt to my feet. "You do this and I'll kill you."

The words were a vow and Kaleb knew it. But his lips twitched. "It's for your own good. Father knows best and all that garbage."

Panic coursed through me as Garrison punched in the code to the cell door. It swung open and he stepped inside, baton in hand. "Don't fight me." He grinned. "I wouldn't want to have to hurt you."

He'd love nothing more. I took up a fighting stance, but movement out of the corner of my eye pulled my attention. The guards had fingers pressed to their earpieces.

One of them sent a furtive glance in Kaleb's direction. "Alpha. The gates have been breached. I'm getting reports of at least a dozen wolves on the north side. More on the west."

Kaleb's eyes flared. "Send out the alert. All enforcers reporting."

I grabbed Rezah's hand. "They're here."

CHAPTER SIX

"Move!" Kaleb barked at me.

I only grinned. "I don't think so."

"Grab her," he ordered Garrison.

Garrison lunged for me, but I was ready. I released Rezah's hand and dodged to my right. He ran smack into the cot, letting loose a creative curse and grabbing his shin.

"For fuck's sake," Kaleb gritted out. He strode into the cell and towards me.

I leapt over the cot, evading his grasp. Time. It was all I needed. I could feel them now. A humming of energy just below my skin. My mates. They were feeding me their power. I didn't know how it was possible without them touching me, but it was happening.

Rowan? Where are you?

Holden's voice sounded clear as day in my head. I wanted to weep at the deep timbre.

Basement. Kaleb and three guards are down here. They have weapons.

We're coming. Just hold on.

A hand locked around my wrist, dragging me towards the cell door. Garrison sneered down at me. "You better be worth it, you little bitch."

"Don't call her a bitch, you overgrown micropenis." Rezah's knee came up, finding purchase right between Garrison's legs.

His eyes went wide with shock and he dropped like a stone, curling into a ball.

"Get up!" Kaleb yelled. "You're an embarrassment."

He shoved me towards the door of the cell, but I grabbed hold of the bars. Using them for balance, I kicked out my foot, landing squarely on Kaleb's chest. He stumbled back a few steps but not far enough.

His lip curled, exposing his lengthening canines. "You'll pay for that."

Energy crackled over my skin. For the first time in over a week, I felt my connection to that golden pool of energy at my core.

Kaleb turned to Garrison, who was pushing to his feet. "Grab her and get to the tunnels."

"Alpha, they've breached the building above."

"Fuck! Are my enforcers worthless?" It was the first time I'd ever seen any hint of panic from Kaleb.

The man behind him who had been offering to break my bond sent a worried glance towards the door. "I didn't sign up for this." He hurried deeper into the basement, to a door I'd never seen before. Seconds later, he disappeared behind it.

Hands gripped my waist and then I was being lifted in the air. Garrison's scent filled my nostrils and had me fighting a wave of nausea.

"Let her go!" Rezah screamed. She kicked at him but

Garrison was faster, leveling his baton on her. He shot an electrical current through Rezah that sent her collapsing to the floor in a seizure.

The level of rage that filled me was unlike anything I'd ever felt before. My hands dug into his shoulders and I let my energy fly.

Then it was Garrison who dropped to the ground. I barely caught myself before hitting the cement floor with him. He twitched and seized.

"What the hell?" a guard barked.

Kaleb's eyes went wide. "Get a shield down here! She's breaking through."

I stretched my fingers, waving them. "What's the matter, *Dad*? Don't want to hang out with me anymore?"

The two guards pulled their weapons.

"Don't shoot her," Kaleb ordered. "Don't Tase her either. It will only feed her power."

"Then what the hell are we supposed to do?" one asked.

Kaleb glanced to the door. "Will, shift. That's our best hope for corralling her."

"She'll still be able to use her gift on me."

"I don't give a damn. Shift."

A second later, the guard was replaced by a gray wolf. The creature snarled in my direction. The sound had my power reacting on instinct. A bolt of energy shot from my palm, striking him in the chest.

He was there one moment and then lifeless on the floor the next. Panic seized me as my hand dropped to my side. The wolf's chest wasn't moving. He was simply gone. Not gone, dead. Because I had killed him.

Pain bloomed on the side of my temple as a fist landed a blow. Stunned, I stumbled and arms locked around me. "Don't fucking move."

I thrashed in Garrison's hold. But my power wouldn't respond, too traumatized by ending a life. Claws lengthened on Garrison's hand and he punched them into my side.

The pain stole my breath. A burning fire ran along my ribs, into my lungs.

Luc was in my mind in an instant. *Rowan!*

Hurry.

His claws tore at my flesh, energy and blood seeping from me. I scratched at his neck and face, but my nails were no match for Garrison's claws.

"Get her to the tunnel," Kaleb shouted, running for the back door.

I couldn't let them take me, couldn't lose my chance to get to my bond. I summoned everything I had and went for Garrison's eyes with my fingers.

He howled in pain but didn't let me go.

A flash of movement caught my attention. A black wolf. Vaughn.

Relief bloomed in my chest. He was here.

Relief quickly transformed to panic as the guard in front of me raised his gun. I screamed with everything I had in me. But it was too late.

CHAPTER SEVEN

THE ENTIRE WORLD SLOWED AROUND ME. MOMENTS punctuated by the beat of my heart. Vaughn leapt into the air, the bullet just missing him and embedding in the wall.

The guard's eyes widened a second before Vaughn was on him. Vaughn didn't hesitate. He sunk his teeth into the guard's shoulder and with a jerk, snapped his neck.

Kaleb ran for the back door, Garrison on his heels with me over his shoulder. I thrashed again, reaching desperately for that golden pool within me. But I couldn't seem to grab hold. My side pulsed with pain, and I could feel my energy slowly draining away.

The door grew ever closer. I clawed at Garrison, but he barely reacted. Then a blur of black fur launched at us, gaining purchase on Garrison's leg. He howled and cried out for help. Kaleb paused for the briefest of moments. His gaze connected with mine, rage blazing in his eyes.

Power surged in my palms. I could do this. Simply end him here and now. He more than deserved it for what he'd done. But the wolf's lifeless eyes flashed in my mind. Nausea swept through me at what I'd done. All it took was that one moment of regret and Kaleb was gone, abandoning his trusted enforcer to certain death.

Garrison's grip on me tightened, and I cried out in pain. Vaughn let out a vicious snarl and tore at Garrison's back with his claws. A moment later, a black and gray wolf bounded through the space, leaping into the fray.

Anson. I would've known those green eyes anywhere.

As his teeth sank into Garrison's side, the enforcer's hold on me loosened and I tumbled to the floor. The impact sent ripples of pain through my entire body. I couldn't hold in my whimper.

The sound only served to enrage Anson and Vaughn. Seconds later, Garrison was ripped limb from limb. My vision blurred as I struggled to hold on to consciousness.

"Ro!" Keene shouted.

I could hear him but couldn't quite make him out.

"Luc! We need you. Holden, get your dad and the medic bag."

Warm hands cupped my face. "God, Ro. Where are you hurt?"

"Side." I was so cold. I shouldn't have a fever anymore. I was touching Keene; our bond had been cemented.

He muttered a curse and low growls sounded behind him. A moment later, Luc's face filled my vision. There was true devastation in his expression. "Rowan."

He scooped me up into his arms. "We need to get out of here. I can't use my gift well enough. The walls are shielded."

"No wonder we couldn't reach her," Keene muttered.

Fire blazed in my side as Lucas carried me towards the door. I couldn't hold in a small, strangled sound.

31

Luc's jaw tightened to granite. "I'm so sorry. We're almost there."

The second we stepped through the door, the worst of my pain melted away. I was floating in a sea of warmth. I let my head loll onto Luc's chest.

A swirl of voices sounded around me, but I struggled to make one out from the next. All I knew was movement and sound and no more pain.

"Lay her down on the blanket. I've got my kit."

"What did they do to her?" Holden's voice held barely-restrained rage. Warm lips ghosted over my temple. "You're safe. We've got you."

"I'm losing power. It's too much pain," Luc said.

"We'll feed you," Anson jumped in. "Grab his shoulders."

Cool hands lifted my shirt, and some part of me recognized Mason. "These gashes are deep. I think her lung is punctured."

"Does she need a hospital?" Holden pushed.

"If I can close the worst of the gashes, her lung should heal on its own with her healing gift. We'll keep a close eye on her and watch her breathing."

Something cold and wet moved along my side. I recognized the pressure of a needle and thread, but there was no pain. Lucas was taking it all.

And I could feel my bond—their energy and our connection flowing through me. Tears tracked down my cheeks.

"She's crying," Vaughn growled.

I tried to force my eyes open to tell him they were from relief. My eyelids fluttered, light bursting through the dark in brief moments.

Anson leaned over me. "Ro? We're here."

There was a brokenness in his tone that had my eyes fully opening. "Anson," I croaked.

"Baby." He dropped to the ground next to me, nuzzling the side of my face.

"I'm okay."

"You're not. There are fucking gashes in your side."

"I'm okay. You found me."

"Not soon enough," Vaughn gritted out.

He was the only one not touching me. I reached a hand out to him. He stared down at it. "I can't, Ro. My emotions are all over the place."

"Please." I needed them. All of them.

Pain flickered across Vaughn's face, but he took my hand in his.

The feeling that flooded me was indescribable. Sparks of warmth and light and love. Such groundedness. More tears slid down my face.

Holden wiped them away with his thumbs. "Ro."

"I'm crying because I'm happy. I'm so happy."

Keene's thumb swept back and forth across my thigh. "How's your pain?"

I looked up at Luc who'd gone a little pale. "I'm good. You don't have to keep taking so much."

A muscle in his cheek fluttered. "I've never felt that level of pain. What did they do to you?"

Garrison's torture flashed in my mind, quickly followed by an image of Rezah crumpling to the floor. "Rezah!" I tried to get up.

"Don't move," Mason ordered. "You could rip your stitches."

"The girl in the cell. You have to help her."

The guys exchanged looks at my panic. Holden gripped my hand. "Ridge has her. She's regaining consciousness now."

More tears came then. She was okay. She'd get to go home. We both would.

I burrowed my face into Anson's neck, breathing him in. The scents of all my mates filled my senses. We were here. Alive, together.

Mason's head lifted as Mac approached. A grimace lined the head enforcer's face. "We lost Kaleb in the tunnels."

Mason's eyes glowed with anger. "How?"

"The place was booby-trapped. We almost lost two enforcers." He shook his head in frustration. "I'm sorry, Alpha. We have no idea where he could've gone."

CHAPTER EIGHT

I WRAPPED ONE ARM AROUND REZAH IN A HUG, CAREFUL not to tug on my stitches. "Thank you for everything."

She squeezed me gently. "It's me who should be thanking you. I can't believe you got us out."

"We got out together."

Rezah sniffed as she let me go and wiped away a stray tear. "I just wish I had been the one to gut Garrison."

"The sight was pretty damn poetic."

One side of her mouth kicked up. "I hope he suffered."

"Not enough," Anson muttered, pulling me back against his chest.

Mason crossed to us, two enforcers in tow. "Rezah, I just spoke with your alpha. He's so relieved you're safe."

"Can I go home now?"

There was such hope in Rezah's voice, it broke my heart.

Mason gave her a warm smile. "Yes. I'm going to have two of my enforcers, Lexi and Jason, drive you. You'll be safe with them."

Rezah sent a cautious look in the enforcers' direction. Lexi beamed at her. "How do you feel about country music? Jason hates it. I was thinking we could annoy him with it the whole way."

Rezah's lips twitched. "I like country."

Jason moaned. "Seriously, Lex? Why are you the worst?"

Lexi held out her hand to Rezah for a high five. "This is going to be fun."

"You have my number," I told Rezah. "Text me."

"You know it. And maybe you can come to Michigan for a visit."

"I'd love that."

Anson held me a little bit tighter at those words, and I knew it would be some time before the guys would be comfortable with me traveling anywhere.

Lexi and Jason guided Rezah towards an SUV. I bit my lip as she disappeared inside. "She'll be okay, right?"

"She'll be fine," Anson assured me.

Mason nodded. "Jason will call as soon as they've arrived."

Still, my stomach twisted. I had no idea how many people Kaleb had working for him. Or how quickly he could recover from this kind of blow to his operation.

"Still no sign of Kaleb?"

Mason shook his head as the rest of the guys approached. "We've got teams out looking for the end of the tunnel system but so far, nothing."

Holden had a dark look on his face. "None of the guards we captured are talking. But most of the shifters working with Kaleb tucked tail and ran."

Vaughn flexed his fingers. "We could get creative on how we get them to talk."

"No." The word was out before I even realized it. "We can't stoop to their level. We aren't torturers."

Vaughn's ice-blue eyes darkened to a shade I'd never seen before as he shared a look with his brother. None of them had pushed to know what had happened to me in the week that I'd been missing, but I'd just let a little too much slip.

Luc moved in, brushing his lips across mine. His warmth seeped into me even with only the barest of touches. "Let's get you home. We can figure out the rest later."

Home. There was nothing I wanted more.

Mason stiffened and Holden was instantly on alert. "What's wrong?"

"Coby and Jaz just dropped out of the pack link."

Keene straightened, slipping his phone from his pocket to check camera feeds. "Anyone else?"

"No one," Mason answered.

Keene swept through different camera angles on his phone. "I don't see any signs of attack."

I gripped Anson's arms as he held me tightly. He dipped his head to take in my face. "What's wrong, Ro?"

My stomach roiled. "It was Jaz."

"What was?" Holden asked.

"She drugged me. I don't know how she got me to Kaleb, but she's the reason I was taken."

Everyone froze.

"What. Did. You. Say?" The fury coming off Holden was a living, breathing thing.

Luc turned, gripping Holden's shoulders. "Dial it back a notch."

"Dial it back? Did you hear her? One of our pack betrayed her!"

I winced at each word.

Luc shoved Holden hard. "Get it together. You aren't helping."

His chest heaved as he turned on his heel and stalked off.

An ache spread inside me. Luc must have felt it instantly because he turned back to me, framing my face with his hands. "He just needs a minute to get himself under control."

"I know." But I didn't like the sensation of Holden walking away. It hurt too much.

Keene moved in close, brushing his lips over my hair. "He blames himself for not watching her more closely."

"It's not his fault," I argued.

Vaughn's gaze followed Holden as he walked towards the woods. "Logic doesn't help in situations like these. The demons take over. And it doesn't help that we could've lost you."

I opened my mind to Holden. *This isn't your fault.*

He was silent for a moment before answering. *I could've stopped it.*

No, you couldn't have. She would've found a way somehow.

I should've been paying closer attention. She was weird after you were taken. Bizarrely helpful.

I couldn't help the low growl that slipped out. I'm sure Jaz was all sorts of helpful. Anything that would get her closer to Holden.

I love you, Ro. Since the moment I met you, you're all I've wanted.

My heart warmed at his words. *I love you too. Come back to me.*

Always. But I need to run off a little of this excess energy. I'm going to join one of the searches for a bit.

Okay. Be safe.

I will.

I blinked a few times, Lucas coming into focus in front of me. His lips curved. "Better?"

I nodded and looked at Mason. "I should've said something as soon as I got out. I honestly forgot until you said her name."

Mason's jaw worked back and forth. "None of this is your fault. There was a lot going on. I'm so sorry, Rowan. I never thought Coby would betray me this way."

"I don't know that she had any part of it—"

"She's hiding her daughter," he growled. "A daughter who tried to assassinate the future Luna of our pack. It's treason."

I swallowed hard. I'd picked up enough over the past few months to know that treason was punishable by only one thing. Death.

Mason shook his head. "I have enforcers searching for them now, and I'll put the word out with other trusted packs. They won't have many options to hide."

I wanted Jaz found. Punished. But I didn't want her dead. I just wanted her incapacitated. Some sort of jail for shifters.

In that moment, the exhaustion hit me. The weight of this past week. All I'd been through. All we'd all been through. My legs began to shake.

Anson swept me up in his arms as gently as possible. "It's time to go."

I leaned into his chest. "Take me home."

CHAPTER NINE

I LOWERED MY T-SHIRT AS MASON SNAPPED OFF HIS medical gloves.

"I can't believe how quickly that healed. Especially given how compromised you were."

Vaughn let out a low growl and shoved off the kitchen island, stalking out of the room.

Keene's gaze tracked his brother. "It's going to take some time for him to move past this."

"For all of us to move past it," Anson muttered as he moved in closer to me in the breakfast nook. "You need to eat more."

I looked down at my mostly empty plate that had housed breakfast for dinner: eggs, bacon, pancakes. I'd packed as much of it away as I could and it had likely helped me heal. But even I recognized that my healing was faster than normal. "I'm full. What I really want is a shower."

Luc held a hand out to me. "Come on. I'll make sure you have everything you need."

"I got it—"

He cut me off with a look. "Let us take care of you. We need it."

I nodded and pushed to my feet.

"I'll go check on Vaughn," Keene said.

My heart ached. We'd all been through so much, and my kidnapping was tearing open the wounds of so many of us.

Luc wrapped an arm around my shoulders. "We'll be okay."

"It doesn't feel that way right now."

He pressed his lips to my temple. "I know. I didn't say it would happen immediately, but we'll get there."

I wanted to believe him but couldn't seem to get myself there. Maybe after a good night's sleep, I'd feel a little more optimistic.

Luc opened the door to my bedroom, and I sighed as my feet sank into the plush carpet. The room had a hint of lavender in the air from the candle by my bed. I couldn't wait to slip beneath those covers and sleep for a week.

Luc ducked into the closet and came back with my coziest pair of pajamas. "Want me to wait in here while you shower?"

I shook my head. "I'll be fine. I just want to get clean." And I needed a few moments alone. Needed to let my guard down so that I didn't have to put on a brave face, knowing how worried the guys were about me.

"Call if you need anything. We'll be right downstairs."

I closed the distance between us, brushing my lips against his and then sinking into the kiss. It was comfort and warmth and a stirring of a brighter heat somewhere down deep. "Love you," I whispered against his lips.

"More than anything."

I stepped back out of Luc's hold and headed for the bathroom. If I didn't walk away then, I'd never make it to the shower.

I stripped off the institutional sweats and T-shirt that had been imposed on me by Kaleb's enforcers and shoved them into the trash can. I would've burned them if I'd had a match or lighter. Turning on the shower, I held a hand under the water until it heated.

Stepping under the spray, I relished the heat. I let it soothe my injured muscles as I massaged shampoo and conditioner into my hair. I inhaled the scent of my favorite rose bodywash as I rubbed it into my skin. My fingers stilled on scar after scar. I'd forever carry these reminders of my sessions with Garrison and his cruelty.

Images flashed in my mind. The panic and fear of never seeing my mates again. A sob tore free from my chest before I knew what was happening. One after the other wracked my body until I was forced to lower myself to the bench in the tiled space.

The bathroom door flew open and then Holden was stepping into the shower in nothing but a pair of basketball shorts. In a flash, he lifted me into his lap. I curled around him, holding tight. Scared that if I let go, he might disappear forever.

He tugged me against him, cocooning me. "I've got you. You're safe."

"I-I was so scared I'd never see any of you again."

For the first time, I gave voice to the fear that had held me captive for eight days. I hadn't let myself speak of it when I was in the cell, too scared that I would bring it into existence with my words. But now I could be honest with myself.

"But you fought your way back to us."

"We fought our way back to each other."

Holden slid his hand along my jaw, tipping my face to his. "And we always will, Rowan."

There was such confidence in those words. I sank into his certainty.

Holden stroked my hip where the bond mark was complete. "We're stronger now. No one can tear us apart."

Each tease of his fingers against my mark sent delicious sparks through me. Before I knew what was happening, my lips were on Holden's. I lost myself in the kiss. It was desperate, almost feral. Need clawed at me. For closeness, for Holden.

He broke away, panting. "Ro, you've been hurt. You need rest."

"I need *you*."

Holden searched my face, looking for some sign.

"Please." I didn't care that I was begging. I needed to feel him inside me. To remind myself that we were both here and alive.

"You have me."

In a flash, he was lifting me with one hand and shucking his shorts with the other. I straddled his lap, sinking down onto his length. I closed my eyes at the stretch, just that hint of pain.

Holden's lips ghosted along my neck as I adjusted to his size. Teasing kisses and nips. Warmth spread through me as his hands found my breasts.

I rocked against him, easing into a rhythm. My mouth found Holden's, and I poured everything I couldn't say into that kiss. Lips, teeth, and tongues gave voice to a language that was our own.

His hips arched up, driving him deeper inside me. I couldn't hold in my moan. But I needed more. I picked up my speed as Holden's thumb circled my clit.

Sensation zinged through me, that cord within me tightening. Holden shifted, going impossibly deeper, hitting that spot that had a cascade of colors dancing behind my eyelids. Energy swirled between us, the final connection sinking deeper into place.

Holden pressed down on that bundle of nerves and that cord frayed, sending me spiraling in light and sensation. A falling apart and coming together. And as I collapsed against Holden, I knew without a doubt he was mine forever.

CHAPTER TEN

HOLDEN PULLED OUT A STOOL AT THE VANITY. "SIT."

I met his eyes in the mirror as I pulled my robe tighter around myself. "You sound like Vaughn with that bossiness."

His lips twitched and he kissed the back of my head. "Please?"

"I take it back. I don't think Vaughn has ever said *please* in his life."

Holden choked on a laugh as he bent to open a drawer. "You've got a point there." As I sat, Holden plugged in a hairdryer. "Do you put anything on your hair before you dry it?"

I opened another drawer and grabbed some hair oil. It was one that Cass had picked out for me and it smelled amazing. I moved to open it, but Holden snatched it out of my hand. "I've got it."

He poured some into his palms and rubbed them together. He worked it through my hair in gentle movements.

"I could get used to this, you know."

Holden grinned at me in the mirror. "I like anything that gets my hands on you."

My face heated as memories of just what his hands could do filled my mind. My belly tightened. How was it possible that I wanted him again already?

Holden let out a low growl. "You keep looking at me like that and we'll never make it out of this bathroom."

I couldn't hold in my laughter. "Sorry."

"You never have to apologize for wanting one of us."

He clicked on the hairdryer and set to work drying my strands. Holden attacked the process like he did everything else, meticulously and with such care. He was so intensely focused on his task, I couldn't help but smile.

There was a reverence in how he worked through it. Never once did he tug too hard or let my strands tangle. He made sure every last piece was completely dry.

It wasn't until the tears fell from my cheeks that I realized I was crying. Holden caught sight of me in the mirror and froze. He quickly shut off the hairdryer and turned me around. "What's wrong?"

I wrapped my arms and legs around him like a monkey clinging to a branch. "I love you."

"And that makes you cry?"

"It's been so long since someone has taken care of me like this." My voice hitched as I struggled to get the words out.

He burrowed his face in the crook of my neck. "Ro."

"I can't tell you what it means to me. I can feel how much you love me."

Holden carried me into the bedroom and set me on the bed, kneeling between my legs. His hands slid along my jaw, cupping my face. "I do. More than I can put into words."

"I'm sorry I held back. I didn't realize it until I was in that cell. I'm the one who kept our bond from forming. I didn't mean to—"

Holden silenced me with a kiss. It was full of tenderness and all the things we struggled to find the words for. "It's okay. We found our way to each other. And sometimes fighting so hard for something makes us appreciate it even more."

I pressed a hand to his bare chest. His steady heartbeat thumped against my palm. "I promise to never take you for granted. To never waste a moment we have together."

His lips brushed against mine again. "Every moment with you is a gift."

My eyes burned, more tears straining to get free. But I forced them down. I'd felt like a leaky faucet ever since I'd made it out of that basement. No more. I wrapped myself around Holden and held on.

I didn't know how long we stayed like that. I didn't hear the door open or footsteps. It was a throat clearing that had me releasing Holden.

Concern lined the planes of Anson's face. "You okay?"

I stood, crossing to him. Anson opened his arms and I sank into his embrace. "I'm okay."

Anson struggled to keep his hold on me gentle. "I'm not feeling like that's the whole truth."

"Anson," Holden said, his voice low.

"Just needing some extra hugs. I want to make sure you're all real." I tried to infuse levity into my tone but knew it came across forced.

I started to release Anson, but he held tight to me. "You hug me as much as you damn well want."

I smiled against his chest. "Love you."

"So much it scares me sometimes."

That fear was a living and breathing thing. Especially when we'd come so close to losing one another.

"We'll fight our way back to each other. Always." I echoed the words Holden had given me earlier, holding tight to their promise.

Anson's lips skimmed over my hair. "How about we don't lose each other at all?"

A soft laugh escaped me. "That sounds like a good plan to me."

He rubbed his hand up and down my back. "You guys better get dressed. Mason wants a meeting."

A little of the levity and reassurance I'd found in Anson's arms slipped away. "Is everything okay?" I pulled back, searching Anson's face for answers.

"I have no idea. He's been on the phone since you guys went upstairs."

I ignored the twisting sensation in my stomach and hurried to my closet. I went for comfort, pulling on a favorite pair of sweats, a T-shirt of Keene's I'd stolen, and a cozy hoodie. By the time I was out, Holden had grabbed clothes from his room as well. He held out a hand to me. I linked my fingers with his and let the buzz of our connection soothe the worst of my worry.

No matter what, we'd face what lies ahead together.

Anson led the way down the hall and towards the stairs. Low voices drifted up from the living room. Four sets of eyes swung to us as we appeared.

Luc scanned my face. He did his best to hide his worry, but I knew it was there. Since our entire bond was complete, I could feel him more. Sense his emotions in the same way he could sense mine, and I had a feeling his connection to me was stronger as well. "Feel better?"

"Holden gave me a full spa treatment."

Vaughn made a scoffing sound.

Holden glared at him. "No need to be jealous now."

"Beauty parlor isn't on my top list of things to do," he bit back.

"Enough," I cut in, staring at Vaughn. "We've all been through a lot these past few days. Let's remember we're all on the same team here."

A muscle in Vaughn's cheek ticked and he looked away.

I rounded the couch and crossed to him. He retreated, but I was faster. I grabbed his hand and squeezed. "A team. That includes you."

"I'm not a great team member."

"Well, maybe it's time to learn."

"Maybe."

I leaned forward and pressed my lips to his shoulder. There were so many words Vaughn wasn't ready to hear from me. So I said them silently, sending invisible promises through that one touch.

When I straightened, my gaze met Mason's. He looked older in that moment. Tired. His pack had suffered blow after blow recently, and it all rested on his shoulders. One look and I knew even more had been heaped onto him.

"I spoke with the Quad. We have a problem."

CHAPTER ELEVEN

VAUGHN STIFFENED NEXT TO ME. HIS MUSCLES WERE strung so tight, I could feel the tension coming off him in waves. "What now?" he growled.

Mason ran a hand through his hair. "I spoke with Gregor, Cinna, and Ivan. They don't believe Kaleb was the one to take Rowan."

"You've got to be fucking kidding me!" Anson exploded.

Luc gripped his shoulder. "Not helping."

Anson shrugged him off. "Don't do that emotion manipulation with me, man."

Luc held his hands up. "Fine. Then dial it back." He inclined his head towards me.

My jaw locked as my back teeth ground together. "I'm not going to break. I can handle Anson being pissed as hell because I am too." I turned to Mason. "Why don't they believe us?"

"They wanted to know that I had gotten visual confirmation of Kaleb on the premises. I couldn't give them that. He disappeared before I set eyes on him."

"Anson and Vaughn saw him. Rowan and that girl, Rezah," Keene argued.

Mason shook his head. "They want sworn testimony from a council member."

"We caught a few of his damn enforcers," Keene pushed.

Mason sighed. "They said those wolves could've acted without Kaleb's permission."

My heart hammered against my ribs, not in fear, but in rage. Kaleb was twisted beyond belief, but the Quad might be worse if they had every intention of letting him get away with this.

"She has scars all over her damn body."

The entire room went still at Holden's words. Fury laced every single one. His hands clenched into fists as his body vibrated with the effort to hold himself back.

"They fucking tortured her. If the Quad won't stand up for Rowan, I'll come for every last one of them."

My chest seized and I was moving before I knew what was happening. In a flash, I was in front of Holden, my hands fisting in his shirt. "Stop. I'm right here. And I'm fine. You can't say things like that." If the wrong person overheard him, Holden could be tried for treason.

Holden's hands stayed clenched at his sides, his body more closely resembling stone than flesh. "You're not fine. I saw the marks on your body. The fucking gashes."

Memories of Garrison's baton hitting my ribs flashed in my mind. The crack of bone. The white-hot pain. His claws slicing into my stomach, my shoulder. Struggling to breathe through the agony. My breaths now came faster and faster, one tripping over the next as I struggled to get my lungs to inflate.

Luc gave Holden a hard shove and then he was in front of

51

me, cupping my face. "Look at me, Ro. You're safe. You aren't there anymore."

My fingers tingled as I battled to suck in air.

"Focus on me." Luc's soothing energy pulled the worst of the anxiety from me. "Follow me."

He motioned with his hand for me to inhale and then exhale. My entire body trembled as I struggled to breathe with Luc.

"That's it. In. Out."

He repeated the movements until I was breathing at a steadier rate. But I couldn't stop shaking. I felt so damn weak as the memories continued to batter at the walls of my mind. The fear that I'd never see my mates again.

Luc scooped me up in his arms and carried me to the couch. He settled me in his lap and cuddled me close. "You're safe."

"Sorry," I croaked.

"You don't have to be fucking sorry," Anson growled as he took the seat next to us and put my legs in his lap.

"I'm the one who's sorry," Holden said, his face ravaged. "I shouldn't have gone there. Not now."

I reached out a hand to him. "It's okay."

Holden strode towards us, sitting on the coffee table and pressing his lips to my palm. "It's not. I just—they hurt you."

"They need to pay." A little of Vaughn's feral edge bled into his words. "They all have to pay."

I closed my eyes for a moment. I couldn't fight all of my mates' anger. It was too much for me to hold, and I was barely holding on as it was. Exhaustion hammered at every part of me.

Keene gripped his brother's shoulder and guided him towards our huddle. "They do need to pay." His thumb swept across my cheek as he stood behind the couch. "But we need to be smart about this. No rash decisions out of anger."

"Keene's right," Mason said. "The Quad are strategic masters. Kaleb has been planning this move for far longer than we knew. We need to look at the long game, not just short-term vengeance."

Vaughn let out a growl.

Mason's head snapped in his direction. "I want that vengeance. Trust me. But I want our people safe. If we attack without the numbers behind us, we'll be decimated. Countless children will lose their parents. Is that what you want?"

A fraction of the tension bled out of Vaughn. "No. But they can't get away with this."

"You're right there." Mason lowered himself into a chair next to the couch. "I need to speak with Cinna and Ivan one-on-one. Feel out where they truly stand. Gregor was far too gleeful at the news of Rowan's attack."

All my mates let out growls at that.

Mason held up a hand to silence them. "Gregor is the worst of them. Greedy, power-hungry, and only out for himself. But he has wielded control of the Quad for decades. It will take a miracle for them to fully break from him. And if he's in league with Kaleb…"

Holden's grip on my legs tightened as his father's words trailed off. "None of the council wants the upheaval that trying a member of the Quad would bring. But if Kaleb has support from the inside? I don't know how we'll get to him."

"We have to understand the plan," I said quietly. "He talked about it some, but I know who would know more."

"Who?" Keene asked.

"My mom."

CHAPTER TWELVE

ANSON DOVE ONTO THE BED, QUICKLY PULLING ME against him. "Never showered so fast in my life."

"And you stole all the damn hot water," Keene muttered as he climbed in on the other side of me.

Luc grimaced down at Keene. "You took my spot."

"You snooze, you lose."

I couldn't hold in my laughter. I turned in Anson's arms so that I was facing Keene and held out a hand to Luc. "There's plenty of room."

"Not where I want," he grumbled as he climbed on the bed.

I locked my fingers with his. "Love you."

His frown melted, and he let a trickle of warmth bleed through from his hand to mine. "Missed you so damn much."

My throat tightened. "I know."

The moment was broken as Holden and Vaughn strode into the room. Vaughn wore a pair of low-slung sweats and Holden perfectly worn flannel pajamas. I swallowed hard. "Hi."

My voice had a little squeak to it. Vaughn's lips twitched at the sound. I patted the bed. "Plenty of room for both of you."

The hint of a smile slipped from Vaughn's lips. "I'm gonna crash on the couch."

My chest tightened. "Please?"

"It's not because I'm holding myself back. I have nightmares. I could hurt one of you without meaning to."

My heart ached for Vaughn. Keeping himself separate as a way of protecting us all. I bit my bottom lip. "I'll miss you."

His expression softened the barest amount. "I'll be right here."

"Not close enough."

Holden climbed into the bed next to Anson. He leaned over and pressed a kiss to my temple. "We'll get there."

I had to hope we would. I wanted all my mates around me. I wanted to know what it was like to sleep in the safety of Vaughn's arms. And more than anything, I wanted to rest without having world-altering things hanging over our heads.

Keene traced circles on my arm. "Are you sure you're up for seeing your mom tomorrow?"

I'd wanted to go tonight, but everyone had put their foot down at that. Mason had argued that we'd need medical supervision for the visit and that wouldn't be possible until tomorrow. But it felt as if we were racing against an invisible clock. One that had started running long ago when none of us had any idea.

"I have to. If anyone knows what Kaleb is up to, it's Abigail." I just hoped we'd be able to decipher her ramblings. She hadn't been informed that I'd been taken, her doctors had been too worried about her mental state. I still wasn't sure what we'd be able to share with her.

Anson's arm wrapped tighter around me. "If you're too tired

tomorrow, we can wait. Or Mason will go and report back. None of this will help if you push yourself too hard."

"I'll be fine after a good night's sleep."

His lips skimmed my ear. "Then let's get you to dreamland."

Holden flicked off the light. "I think we could all use a little of that."

I thought it would be hard to fall asleep after the adrenaline dump of the past twenty-four hours, but unconsciousness pulled me under almost instantly. Only it wasn't a sea of nothingness that greeted me.

I was back in the cell. The dank smell filled my nostrils. My bare feet padded on the cement floor. I searched for Rezah but she wasn't there. I was completely alone.

"Hello?" I called.

My voice echoed off the cinder block walls. But there was no answer.

Panic grabbed hold, my heart rate picking up as I moved towards the door. I tried to open it but only got a rattle of metal.

A laugh sounded from down the hall, dark and menacing. "I'll always find you, daughter. You can never truly get away."

Kaleb said "daughter" as if I were a possession, not a living, breathing human being.

He held up a hand and one of the batons that Garrison had been so fond of appeared in his grasp. "Did you miss this?"

I fought the urge to shudder. This wasn't real. I told myself the same thing over and over. I tried to remember what I had read about how to wake yourself up from a dream. The first thing was to acknowledge it. "This is a dream."

Kaleb grinned. "It is."

He looked too happy. Almost gleeful.

56

"A special dream."

My stomach sank. "What do you mean?"

He waved a hand at the cell door and it opened. "It means I can do this."

Kaleb leveled the baton at me. Electricity crackled, striking across the space and landing square in my chest. The force of the blow sent me crumpling to the floor. Blinding pain coursed through my muscles. I couldn't hold in my scream.

"Sever your bond."

"No," I croaked, barely able to get the single word out.

He shot another blast into my shoulder. "Break it!"

I rolled to my side, writhing in pain. White dots danced in front of my eyes. Wake up! I ordered myself over and over. But I couldn't seem to climb out of this hell.

"I will cause you more pain than you can fathom. I will destroy your mind one piece at a time until there's nothing left of you for your bond to recognize. I will—"

His words cut off as I gasped into consciousness again. Five pairs of hands held me, and Keene was yelling my name.

My entire body shook. My chest burned as if I'd been branded. I struggled to undo the buttons on my pajama top.

"What the hell was that?" Anson barked.

I had to see. To know if it was real.

Luc moved in closer, covering my hands with his. "What do you need?"

"M-my shirt."

He carefully undid the top three buttons.

An audible gasp sounded around the room. Because right there on my chest was a black spiderweb burn. I had thought I was safe. I wasn't safe at all.

CHAPTER THIRTEEN

"**W**ALK US THROUGH IT AGAIN," HOLDEN SAID AS he paced back and forth across the kitchen.

I rubbed at the spot on my chest. It still ached, but the mark from the blast was fading. "It seemed like a normal dream at first—"

"You mean nightmare," Anson muttered as he leaned against the island.

Holden sent him a quelling look and nodded at me to continue.

"I was back *there*. Only I was alone this time." That had been what first set my panic in motion. Being so completely isolated. "I heard footsteps and Kaleb appeared. It was weird. Some parts of the dream were so realistic and others seemed to be magic. He made that baton appear out of thin air."

I shivered and Luc wrapped his arm around me, pulling me close. "You're safe now."

Keene pushed my mug of tea closer. "Have some more of this."

I wrapped my hands around the mug but didn't drink. "He pulled me into the dream somehow."

Holden and Vaughn shared a look.

"What?"

Holden ran a hand through his hair. "There is a gift that can control dreams. It's rare and to manipulate someone without their permission is against our laws. But I've never heard of someone being physically harmed in a dream."

I swallowed, my throat sticking on the movement. "He said he could break me. Destroy my mind."

A muscle in Vaughn's cheek fluttered wildly. "He's not going to get the chance to do that."

"I can't stay awake forever." That would break my mind just as quickly.

Keene traced circles on my knee. "You woke up as soon as we were all touching you. I have a feeling that gives you some sort of protection."

My gaze lifted to Vaughn. Shadows danced in his eyes. "I'm sorry. I should've stayed closer."

"Don't you dare apologize for him. Kaleb is the one responsible, no one else."

Vaughn's jaw worked back and forth. "There are other protections we can put in place too."

"Like the crystal you gave me?"

I hadn't had a bad dream in so long, I'd hung it on my vanity instead. But it clearly needed to go back under my pillow.

He shook his head. "I don't think that's strong enough."

"Keene's right," Holden said. "Our best line of defense is being together. There's something about our bond that shields Rowan."

Luc's fingers tangled in my hair. "We need to look over the old histories, see if we can find anything about this."

"Kaleb could be mixing gifts with dark magic," Vaughn suggested.

His words had a memory flashing in my mind. "There was a man with Kaleb the day you rescued me. I think he was a witch. They were going to forcibly break the bond because I'd been so sick."

Anson let out a low growl. "I thought witches and warlocks stayed far away from shifters."

Holden scrubbed a hand over his jaw. "Usually, they do. There have been tensions between our groups for centuries, but money can be a powerful motivator."

"The man said something about being paid even if he didn't break the bond."

More low growls sounded at my words.

"If we could find evidence of Kaleb trying to strengthen gifts with dark magic, the Quad would have to act," Keene said.

Anson pushed off the island and began to pace. "And just how are you going to find that? I doubt the warlock is going to come before the Quad and council out of the goodness of his heart."

I pressed myself closer to Keene's side. "We're just throwing out ideas. Let's all take a breath."

Some of the tension bled from Anson and he glanced at Keene. "Sorry, man. I just—"

Keene raised his hand, cutting him off. "I know. We're all worried. And you're right, finding that kind of proof is probably impossible."

"What we need to focus on right now is keeping Rowan safe," Vaughn said.

Another shiver slid through me at the thought of trying to sleep. At knowing Kaleb could be lurking just on the other side of unconsciousness. I rubbed at the spot on my chest again.

Luc's hand covered mine. "Does it still hurt?"

Any hint of discomfort was pulled from me, replaced by warmth. I leaned into him. "You don't have to do that."

"Yes, I do." His hand tightened around mine a fraction. "You were in so much pain. But I couldn't break into the dream. It was like when you were taken. The shields were too strong."

There was such pain in Luc's voice. I moved on instinct, wrapping myself around him and practically climbing into his lap. "I'm okay."

"But you almost weren't."

A pang lit along my sternum. I'd come so close to losing Luc. To losing all of them. And it had marked us all. It didn't help that the hits just kept coming.

"You got to me. Every time, you've come for me."

"Rowan." His voice cracked.

"Every time. You've always been there for me. More than anyone else in my life." My hands fisted in his T-shirt, and I pressed my lips to his neck. "And I know you'll be there for me every day from now on."

"Damn straight," Anson muttered.

Keene let out a soft chuckle as his hand trailed up and down my back. "Rowan's right. No matter what, we find a way."

Luc's lips ghosted over my forehead. "I don't want you in pain, not ever."

It was the worst thing imaginable for my empath. He would feel it more than I ever would. I ran my hand through his hair. "Life will always have pain. But I have you to help me deal with it. As long as I have our bond, I can beat anything that comes my way."

CHAPTER FOURTEEN

ANSON LAID A HAND OVER MINE, STILLING MY fidgeting. "It'll be okay."

I looped my thumb over the top of his hand, holding on. I'd take every tether to them I could get. As we'd made breakfast and gotten ready to go see Abigail, I'd found myself needing to touch at least one of my mates at all times. Fear that Kaleb might be able to reach me even in wakefulness had taken root.

Keene turned onto a smaller back road, guiding the massive SUV around a bend. My stomach dipped as the hospital came into view.

Anson squeezed my hand again. "You don't have to go in. We can talk to her without you."

I shook my head. "I want to go too."

Want wasn't exactly the right word. Need was more accurate. If I let myself cower now, I'd never get back up. I had to keep moving forward.

"We'll be with you the whole time," Holden said, his hand slipping under my hair.

Mason turned in his seat up front. "Her doctor assured me she's more stable than your last visit."

I swore I could still hear Abigail's screams in my mind. I couldn't help the shiver that coursed through me.

Luc's hands found my shoulders, letting in a trickle of his soothing energy. "We'll get through it no matter what. Together."

My gaze traveled to Vaughn sitting beside Luc in the third row. He hadn't said a word as we were getting ready to leave, he had simply climbed into the SUV. Vaughn wasn't pretty words and easy reassurances. He communicated everything he had to say with silent action. And today he was telling me that he was here, a real part of the bond.

I lifted an arm over the seat and rested my hand on his knee, squeezing gently. Vaughn's eyes fixed on the contact. He didn't reciprocate, but he didn't move away either. It was our own form of progress.

Keene pulled into a parking spot at the front of the hospital. The little peace and reassurance I'd felt melted away. I focused on keeping my breathing even, on not allowing my anxiety to get a foothold. All I could do was put one foot in front of the other.

We piled out of the SUV and started towards the front doors. Mason led the way, the guys surrounding me as if someone might jump out at any moment to try and snatch me away. Just as we reached the steps, the door opened. A woman in scrubs smiled at us. "Dr. Barton and Abigail are around back on the patio. Dr. Barton thought the fresh air and open spaces might be good."

Mason dipped his head in a nod. "Thank you."

The woman guided us around the massive building to a beautiful stone patio that overlooked a series of gardens. My steps faltered as I caught sight of Abigail. She faced away from us, standing at an easel, paintbrush in hand. As I moved closer, I could see just how talented she was.

My fingers twitched at my sides. My pull to create had come from the woman who had given me life. But I wasn't nearly as talented as she was. I couldn't help but wonder if that would've been different if Abigail had raised me. Would my artistry be leaps and bounds ahead of where it was now? Would we have spent afternoons walking through museums or bringing landscapes to life?

My heart ached at all the what-ifs. Luc's hand came to the small of my back, that familiar warmth flooding me. I looked up at him and shook my head. "I need to feel it."

He frowned and I couldn't help but smile. I reached up and rubbed at the little lines between his brows. "Tell you what. Let me feel everything right now, and you can put me in a good feels coma on the way home."

Anson moved in closer to my other side. "I know something that would put you in a good feels coma that's a hell of a lot more fun than whatever magic mojo Luc has planned."

I snorted and smacked his stomach. "We're about to talk to my mother. Please don't make sex jokes."

His lips skimmed the shell of my ear. "But I love making you blush."

I shivered again, but this time, the sensation was more than pleasant.

Keene grinned at me. "I'll give it to Anson. He's good with distractions."

"The best," he quipped back.

I rolled my eyes. "No ego either."

Our steps slowed as we reached the patio. Dr. Barton rose

and gave us warm smiles. "Welcome." Her gaze landed on me, concern filling her eyes. "How are you feeling, Rowan?"

"Better." I couldn't give her more than that. The roller-coaster ride of the past forty-eight hours would take days to explain.

"I'm glad to hear it." She glanced over her shoulder at my birth mother. "Abigail is doing much better too." Her gaze came back to our group and settled on Mason. "The painting was an excellent idea. We've had a number of breakthroughs since implementing it."

Mason rubbed at the back of his neck, as if uncomfortable with Dr. Barton's praise. "I'm glad it's helping. I just remembered how she was always happiest with a paintbrush in her hand."

Dr. Barton nodded. "I've taken to giving her pastels in our sessions so that she can sketch while we talk. It has kept her calm, and the drawings give her another way to communicate with me."

I looked at the painting Abigail was creating now. It was of the gardens in front of us, but more. Within the gardens were wolves in battle. Lightning and sparks of energy dotted the sky. But it was beautiful.

I stepped forward, coming to stand next to her as she layered in storm clouds. "This is amazing."

Abigail studied the painting. "I'm rusty."

The laugh that came to my lips was nothing but authentic. "If this is rusty, then you really put my skills to shame."

She turned towards me. "Rowan." Her gaze skimmed over me and then she froze. She dropped her paintbrush and pressed her hand to my chest, eyes going wide. "He marked you."

CHAPTER FIFTEEN

M Y HEART POUNDED AGAINST ABIGAIL'S HAND. "M-marked?"

She tugged at my flannel shirt, exposing the barest hint of a black mark. "You have to get it off you."

My entire bond had moved closer, but it was Luc who actually stepped up next to me. "What does the mark mean?"

His voice was the gentlest probe. Abigail released her hold on me and stepped back, wringing her hands. "He'll always know where to find you now. As long as it's present."

That wasn't great news, but I wasn't exactly hiding either. "I'll be okay. It's fading," I assured her.

Tears filled her eyes. "I didn't want this for you."

"Want what?"

"You're the only one who can stop him. Only you. He's gotten too strong." Abigail's fingers tapped a rapid beat against her thigh.

Mason bent and picked up her paintbrush. He kept his movements slow and exaggerated so that he wouldn't startle her, but he wrapped Abigail's fingers around the brush and turned her back to the painting. "Is he using dark magic?"

Abigail began to paint again, her strokes more aggressive than they'd been before. "It stains his soul. Turns it black."

"But I can stop him?"

I could feel the energy of the guys behind me. Worry. Protectiveness. Rage. Now that the bond was complete, I could sense it all. So much more than the brief *knowings* I'd gotten before.

Abigail darkened the sky above one wolf with a silver-gray coat. I had to assume it was Kaleb. There was a cruelty in the wolf's eyes that I recognized. She swirled the angry clouds spilling out of him. "Kaleb's shields can only be broken by one who bends our very life force."

"An energy bender?" Holden pushed.

Abigail's head bobbed up and down as she moved her brush to the girl with her arms extended. "You're the only one who can break through."

"Stop it." Vaughn's words snapped out.

Abigail's head jerked in his direction and paint flew.

I gaped at him. "Vaughn—"

"She's not telling you the most important thing. Energy benders and those in their bonds can sometimes break through shields. But if an energy bender pushes too far, it could kill them."

Everyone went silent. The only sound was a faint rustling of leaves in the trees.

Holden shifted in Vaughn's direction. "How do you know that?"

"I read those damn journals you have when I can't sleep. The ones from generations ago. There's a whole section on this shit." He scowled at Abigail. "Rowan's not going down that road."

I bristled at that. "Excuse me?"

Vaughn's ice-blue eyes flashed with heat. "You don't get to kill yourself because of your gift."

"You don't think I can do it." It hurt more than I wanted to admit that Vaughn didn't believe in me.

He moved in a flash, his hands coming up to frame my face. "I think you can do anything. That doesn't mean the risks are worth it. Breaking shields requires physical and mental strength. Some of these energy benders trained for years and still died trying to do it."

I shoved down that flash of panic that rose in the back of my throat. "Then I'll have to train harder. Smarter. I have you guys. You make me stronger."

"It's the bond of six that could save you," Abigail said softly, more tears filling her eyes. "It was always your destiny. I didn't want it for you. I wanted you to be safe. To have a normal life."

This woman had given up everything to keep me safe. It had broken her in more ways than I could ever imagine. I met her eyes. "Thank you. For everything you did—"

"I'd take it for you," she cut in. "I'd take your burden in a second."

"I know you would." It was the first time in so long that I'd felt loved by a parent. And that alone was a gift. "You can tell me what I need to know."

Abigail scanned the forests around us as she swallowed. "He wants to rule. Thinks he can be king."

"He told me that." And I'd filled Mason and the guys in on all of Kaleb's delusions of grandeur.

Abigail gripped her paintbrush harder. "He thinks shifters with no powers should be our slaves. Slaves or killed altogether."

Anson stiffened behind me. "He can't be serious."

"Kaleb sees them as less than us. Weakening us. But really he wants control and power. He wants to pull the strings and exert his will. It's all he's ever cared about."

I felt that from him. In the basement and in that dream. He truly didn't understand how someone wouldn't come to see things his way.

Keene moved closer to Abigail, pulling out his phone. "Do you have any idea where he might be holed up?"

She shook her head back and forth in jerky movements. I thought for a moment that she might lose it, but Abigail closed her eyes and let out a shaky breath. "I only went to a place a few hours from here."

"In eastern Washington?" Keene asked.

She nodded. "There wasn't much there. Just a couple of buildings. One made of cinder block walls."

I couldn't help the tremor that ran through me. I didn't want to ever see those kinds of walls again.

Keene looked at Abigail, doing his best to keep his expression gentle. "We've found that one. Anywhere else he mentioned liking especially?"

She tapped her fingers against her lips. "Idaho. He talked about going to this lake in Idaho with his dad. He said he was going to buy it one day. What was the name?" Her words trailed off as she tried to recall, the tapping of her lips growing more intense. She let out a growl. "I can't remember. There were mountains there, I know that."

Keene shoved his phone back into his pocket. "That's okay. It's enough to start looking."

Abigail turned to me, a tear sliding down her cheek. "You'll have to be stronger than you ever thought possible."

"I can do it." I wasn't sure if that was true, but I knew I'd give my all to try. I wouldn't let Kaleb commit to what could amount to genocide. Subjugation. Torture. Heat rose in me, a little of that anger growing into a flame.

"I know you can." Abigail stared straight at me, eyes unblinking. "Kaleb received a prophecy from a seer when he was younger."

My vision went blurry at the edges. "What did they say?"

"The one of your blood will help you rise to untold power. Or take the breath from your lungs."

CHAPTER SIXTEEN

THE WORDS SCRAWLED IN THE JOURNAL BLURRED AND I rubbed at my eyes. Story after story had embedded itself in my brain. Ones where energy benders had pushed themselves too far. Ones where their minds were left in tatters. Ones where their bodies were broken. Or worst of all, ones where they ceased to exist completely.

Some energy benders wanted to break shields simply for the challenge, to prove their dominance. They loved that they were revered and feared, and only wanted to build on that lore. But others were only trying to survive.

I squinted at the scrawl on the page. The paper had turned yellow with age. Yet I could feel this woman's pain as if it were my own. Cara was trying to defend her pack from another that wanted their lands. The attacking pack had a shield and fire wielder, and the woman knew if she didn't break through the shield, they would decimate her family, her bond, everyone.

My heart ached for her as I read her words. Cara recounted her training regime in detail. She talked about what she thought helped and what was a waste of time. I flipped the page in my notebook, jotting down more ideas.

I was surprised at how much the physical contributed to the mental. Cara talked about how important balance seemed to be, within her bond and within her own body. Her strength and endurance needed to grow to keep up with her gift.

Sports had never been my forte, but I'd always been fond of those Olympic training montages they showed during coverage of the games. I'd need to channel some of that grit if I had a prayer at succeeding.

A flood of anxiety swamped me as Abigail's words played in my mind. *The one of your blood will help you rise to untold power. Or take the breath from your lungs.* I swallowed against the lump in my throat as my grip on my pen tightened.

The chair next to me scraped against the floor and I jumped. So much for my ninja skills developing simply by reading the pages of a journal.

Anson looked down at my research. His brows lifted as he scanned the items on my list. "That's a hell of a workout."

I closed the notebook. "The more I read, the more I realize how important the physical piece of this is."

His lips pressed into a firm line.

"What?"

"I just don't want you pushing yourself too hard, too quickly. You've been through a lot in the past couple of weeks. Your body needs time to heal."

I did my best not to bristle at Anson's concern. I knew it came from a good place, but I didn't have time to waste. "Super healer, remember?"

"It's more than just healing injuries. You need rest and to let your mind heal too."

I swallowed down the growl that wanted to surface. "Time is the one thing we don't have. We have no idea when Kaleb is going to make another move. I have to be ready."

My heart rate kicked up as I heard Abigail's words echo in my brain yet again. They'd been on a constant loop since we'd left the hospital.

Anson's hand closed around mine as he loosened my grip on the pen. It clattered to the table. "Talk to me, Ro."

My eyes burned, a combination of fatigue and tears trying to break free. "What if I'm like him?"

Anson stilled. "What?"

"He's my father. Half of my genetic makeup is from him."

Anson grabbed hold of my chair and turned me to face him. He pulled me in close, his legs going to the outside of my own. "You are *nothing* like him."

"The prophecy. It says I could help him reach untold power."

"Or you could steal the breath from his lungs."

I stared down at my hands. Hands that had the power to kill. That had killed. "I can do horrible things."

Anson framed my face with his hands. "You can do amazing things. You can protect yourself. Protect others. There is no one on this planet that I would trust with this power more than you."

A single tear slipped free and Anson swiped it away with his thumb. I leaned into him, my head dropping to his shoulder. Anson's arms went around me, his fingers traveling up and down the ridges of my spine. "There is so much light in you. There's a reason fate gave you this gift. Trusted you with it."

"I'm scared I'll make a wrong choice or won't be ready, and because of me, he'll win."

Anson's fingers came up along the column of my neck, finding that spot he loved. "This isn't on your shoulders alone. We've learned time after time, we're stronger when we're together. Lean into that. Lean into *us*. We want to help you."

"She said it has to be me that ends him."

Anson's hand tightened the barest amount on my neck, his jaw locking. "That might be true, but you won't be doing it alone. You aren't alone anymore."

Hints of anger bled through Anson's words. I pulled back, taking in the same heat lacing his green eyes. "I know I'm not."

"Do you? As soon as we got home, you holed up with these damn journals and didn't say a word. You locked us out."

And that had hurt him. He had lived his life so isolated before the bond formed, with a mother who hadn't even cared that he'd moved out of their home, and a father who hadn't wanted anything to do with him. And I had dug a knife into those wounds today.

I moved on instinct, all but launching myself at him. "I'm so sorry. I didn't mean to push you out. I should've realized—"

Anson didn't cut me off with words. He stole anything else I was going to say with his mouth. A kiss that was a mix of anger and need. And I took it all.

CHAPTER SEVENTEEN

WE DIDN'T NEED WORDS. WE NEEDED TOUCH AND connection. To tell each other how we felt with our bodies.

Anson lifted me, and my legs wrapped around his waist. A moment later, he was shoving journals and papers off the dining table and lowering me to it, but I didn't lose his mouth for a second. I swallowed his hurt and anger, but it was his need that drove me higher.

I could feel the desperation coming off him in waves. How much he needed to feel that connection with me. Pricks of guilt gnawed at me, but I shoved them aside, focusing only on Anson.

He grabbed hold of my tank top, tugging it over my head. Then his lips were closing around my nipple. The scorch of sensation was instantaneous, from the peaks of my breasts to the depths of my core.

My legs tightened around Anson as his teeth grazed my nipple. His length pulsed beneath his sweats as I pulled him closer to me, needing to feel so much more. Needing to feel everything.

"Anson." His name on my lips was more a breath than an

actual word, but it seemed to snap something in Anson. His hands went to my sleep shorts, and a second later there was nothing but cool air against my overheated flesh.

Then his mouth was at the apex of my thighs. There was no delicate exploration, Anson just took. His tongue drove into me with thrust after thrust, then came to my clit, circling and sucking deep.

I let out a mewling sound and my hands gripped his shoulders. Just as I grabbed hold of one sensation, another found me. Anson's fingers slid inside me, curling and twisting. Each new movement tightened something inside me.

"Don't come." He growled the order against that bundle of nerves.

"Please." I wasn't above begging.

"Need to feel you come around my cock."

My hips lifted of their own volition, seeking more of everything he was giving me.

Anson chuckled against my skin. "Looking for something?"

"You. Always you."

It was all he needed. In a flash, his sweats were gone and he was lifting me off the dining table and turning me around. "Hold on."

I gripped the edge of the wood, and seconds later, Anson thrust inside me. Each movement poured all that emotion into me. I met him thrust for thrust. The frustration and anger transforming into something more. It was that desperate need I'd felt earlier, but there was fear there too. Anson needed to know that I was with him. That I was alive and strong.

I arched my back as he slammed into me, impossibly deeper.

I felt everything he couldn't say. And matched him every step of the way.

My walls tightened around him and Anson growled, picking up his pace. His hand came around, finger circling my clit. He pressed down and I fractured. Every part of me shattered as sensation swept over me in waves.

The world was awash in light, in color, and I was suddenly weightless. There was nothing but me and Anson and the energy we created together.

As I came back to myself, I realized Anson was holding me up because I'd completely collapsed and would've face-planted on the table. His chest heaved as he straightened, keeping me against him. His lips trailed down the column of my throat. "Love you, Rowan."

I leaned into the contact. "I love you too. I'm so sorry I made you feel like I was shutting you out."

He grinned against my skin. "I don't feel that way anymore."

I couldn't hold in my laugh. Anson groaned. "You're going to kill me."

I winced as he slipped from my body. Anson froze. "Are you hurting? Was that too much?"

Turning to face him, I wrapped my arms around his neck. "You are never too much. It was perfect."

He lifted me into his arms, carrying me out the back door to an outdoor shower that was around the corner from the hot tub. He turned the spray to warm and stepped under it with me still in his arms.

I might've told him I was fine, but Anson clearly felt the need to take care of me. There was a gentleness in his movements that made my heart ache. I couldn't help the moan that slipped from my lips as he shampooed my hair.

"You keep making sounds like that and you're gonna kill me all over again."

My gaze traveled down to his length. Just looking at it made my thighs clench.

"Rowan," he growled.

I quickly looked away. "Sorry."

"Insatiable," he muttered as he rinsed my hair.

"Not sorry for that."

Anson kissed the side of my neck. "Nor should you be."

I turned to face him as he worked conditioner into my hair. "Are you okay?" I asked softly.

He nodded. "I guess I don't do well feeling disconnected from you."

It made sense with all he'd been through. But it would also be a challenge with the bond. There were so many moving pieces, and I needed to be diligent about making sure we all felt in tune with one another.

I filled my hand with bodywash and lathered it into Anson's skin. "Any time you feel that way, just tell me."

The corner of his mouth kicked up. "You mean use my words instead of being a growly asshole?"

Laughter bubbled out of me. "Well, I mean, I didn't mind the table portion of the evening. But I hate that I hurt you. I never want to do that."

"It's going to happen. It's how we deal with the hurt that counts."

I rinsed the soap from Anson's chest as he lifted my hair to the spray. "I know you're right. I just hate the idea of you hurting."

"Not hurting anymore."

"Good."

He rubbed bodywash gently over my back and arms. "But I want in on your plans."

"That's fair. How do you feel about a run and a workout before school tomorrow?"

Anson groaned. "Why'd you have to start with something at the crack of dawn?"

"Hey, you wanted to be included."

He grimaced as he washed the soap away. "Fine."

Anson shut off the water and grabbed two towels from a shelving unit built into the side of the house. He wrapped one around me, pulling it tight, then patted himself dry and wrapped that towel around his hips. I'd never get tired of having his golden skin on display.

He pressed a quick kiss to my lips as he ushered me inside. "We better get to bed if you're getting us up early."

Our footsteps slowed as we walked inside. There were pieces of clothing and papers everywhere. It looked as if a tornado had passed through the center of the room. I couldn't hold in my laughter. "Maybe we should clean this up first."

CHAPTER EIGHTEEN

A FEW BROWS ROSE AS ANSON AND I WALKED INTO the bedroom. Luc stifled a chuckle. "Did a pipe burst somewhere?"

"Something like that," Anson muttered under his breath.

My face flamed and I smacked him in the stomach.

He grinned. "What? A pipe did burst."

I covered my face with my hands as Keene chuckled and pulled me into a hug. "Don't be embarrassed. We should all be having fun whenever we can. We need to let off steam."

Anson and I had certainly done that. I ducked out of Keene's hold and headed for the closet, mumbling something about needing pajamas. I shoved the clothes Anson had torn from my body into my hamper and then hurried to pull on fresh sleep shorts and a tank. By the time I made it back out to the bedroom, Anson had found a pair of pajama bottoms.

All the guys hovered around the bed. Lucas had propped himself against the pillows. Holden sat on the edge of the mattress. Vaughn paced.

I swallowed hard as I looked past Keene and Anson, who

stood between me and the place I'd loved until last night. Before I knew sleep could pull me into a battle for my life.

Holden stood, crossing to me. His hands slid along my jaw and into my hair. "We won't let him get to you."

"How?"

Luc sat up. "If we're all touching you while you sleep, Kaleb shouldn't be able to break through."

"You guys can't stay awake all night just so I can sleep." They needed their rest too. We'd all been burning the candle at both ends for weeks.

"We can," Vaughn gritted out.

Keene stepped forward, holding up what appeared to be bathrobe ties. "But we won't have to."

Anson grinned. "Kinky. I like it."

I scowled at him. "Not helping."

He just winked at me.

Keene rolled his eyes. "Here's how it'll work. I'll tie our hands together. Holden and Luc will lay in between us. It'll keep our arms over the two of them so there's contact. Then Anson can lay on your other side and—"

"I'll sit at the end of the bed and hold onto your leg," Vaughn cut in.

"You can sleep in the bed with the rest of us—"

He shook his head, halting my words. "This works."

A pang lit along my sternum. I didn't want to be disappointed at Vaughn holding himself back from us, but I couldn't help it. I shoved the hurt down and nodded. "Whatever you're comfortable with."

Something that looked a lot like regret passed over his features. "It's for the best."

But how did Vaughn truly know that? He hadn't let himself try. I bit my tongue and climbed onto the mattress. Luc curved himself around me. His lips grazed my ear. "Give it time."

I nodded but didn't say a word. I couldn't give voice to hopes that I wasn't sure would come to fruition.

Holden climbed in, Luc and Keene behind him. As Anson lowered himself to my other side, Luc tied Keene's and my hands together. This way, I could move my other arm and wouldn't feel trapped but had contact with everyone.

"Wait. Anson, hand me my phone?" I asked.

He grabbed the device on the nightstand and passed it to me. I quickly set my alarm and handed it back. "Thanks."

Anson plugged it in as Vaughn untucked the blankets at the end of the bed. A pleasant shiver skated up my spine as his fingers curled around my ankle. Now that our entire bond was cemented, I no longer felt physical pain when Vaughn kept his distance. But when I got that contact, everything in me flared to life with rightness. It felt so good, it almost hurt. Because I knew it wouldn't last.

Concern lined Anson's face as he lowered himself to the pillows. "You okay?"

I nodded. Just terrified my father would murder me in a dream or Vaughn would break my heart beyond repair.

His lips pressed together in a firm line and I knew he must've felt some of my worry.

As Keene shut off the light, Holden leaned over and pressed a kiss to my bare shoulder. "We'll keep you safe."

They would try. But I wasn't sure it would be enough.

The angry blare of an alarm pulled me from sleep, followed by a series of groans. My arm ached from being held in the same position all night tied to Keene's.

"Someone turn that fucking thing off," Vaughn barked from the end of the bed.

Anson felt around for my phone and finally shut off the sound.

"What time is it?" Holden mumbled.

Luc rubbed at his eyes. "It isn't even light out."

I loosened the tie on my wrist and slid towards the end of the bed, careful to avoid Vaughn. "Go back to sleep."

All of the guys' eyes came to me.

Keene sat up. "Where are you going?"

"For a run."

Anson moaned but got to his feet. "I'm coming."

I almost laughed at the pout on his face.

Holden scrubbed a hand over his face. "And why are you going for a run before it's light out?"

The humor I'd felt at Anson's sulking fled at Holden's question. "We're running out of time. Mason said we have to go back to school today, so it's now and after classes. I need to make use of the windows I have."

His jaw tightened, but he slid towards the end of the mattress. "We'll all go."

"You don't have to—"

"Together," Luc cut me off. "You train, we train. The physical workouts will help us too. The empath who told me how to work at breaking through shields says it helps."

I straightened, ears perking up at that. I'd never asked how

Luc had been able to reach me while I was being held by Kaleb. "Who taught you?"

Wariness filled Holden's expression. "An old, crazy shifter."

"She's not crazy," Luc defended.

Holden arched a brow.

Luc flushed. "Okay, she's a little eccentric, but what she said was true." He turned back to me. "She told us to link our powers and hold an image of you in our minds. It took everything we had, but I could reach you in small bursts and eventually help you connect to Holden."

An image of them exhausted and scared out of their minds filled my thoughts. I crossed to Luc, throwing my arms around him. "Thank you."

He nuzzled my neck. "We'll fight with everything we have for you."

I knew it was the truth. And it was what scared me most of all.

CHAPTER NINETEEN

I STARED AT THE BRICK BUILDING AS ANSON PULLED INTO his parking spot. Classes, studying, and high school drama felt like another lifetime. One where I wasn't concerned about a sociopath of a bio dad and learning how to harness a power that could kill me.

Keene's thumb traced circles on my knee. "You okay?"

That wasn't a word that felt like it applied to me. I was exhausted down to my bones. It was more than a physical exhaustion, though that was certainly a piece of it. We'd done a run to the gym down by the main lodge, a workout there, then shifted to run back home in our wolf forms.

My wolf stirred inside me at the memory. She loved running with her mates, feeling the freedom of finally stretching her legs after the drugs Kaleb had given us had kept her suppressed. As much as that time had fed my soul, it had taken it out of me. It would take time to build up the endurance I'd need.

Keene squeezed my thigh. "Ro?"

"I'm good. What excuse did Mason give them this time?"

Holden shifted in the front seat so he was facing me. "Death in the community."

My lips thinned. There had been death. Thankfully not on our side, but a handful of shifters had lost their lives when the Ridgewood pack had shown up to rescue me. And for what? Some madman's quest for ultimate power. It made me nauseous.

Luc brushed the hair away from my face. "We can take another day if you need it. Mason can tell the school it was too soon for us to return."

"No. The longer we wait, the worse it'll be." The more stares and whispers we would get. That feeling would never sit right with me. Would always grate against my skin in a painful burn. It was tied so closely to what I'd experienced after losing Lacey. Today would be the worst of it. If I could make it through today, everything would be fine.

"If anyone's an asshole, I'll deck them," Anson said as he shut off the SUV.

Holden groaned. "Not the solution."

"Maybe not, but it'll make me feel a hell of a lot better."

My lips twitched. I couldn't help it. I leaned forward and kissed his shoulder. "Love you."

He bent, brushing his lips against my temple. "More than anything."

My heart gave an almost painful squeeze. But it was a good kind of pain. The type that made you realize how lucky you were.

Keene opened his door and slid out, offering me a hand. The second my feet touched the cement, a tiny body slammed into me. I scented Cass before I even had a chance to make out her blonde hair. She squeezed me hard. "I'm so glad you're okay. I wanted to come see you yesterday, but my guys said you needed to rest. Are you okay? You're not hurt, are you? I'd like to junk punch Kaleb—"

I cut her off, hugging her back as tightly as I could manage. "I'm fine."

Jack sent me a kind smile. "She missed you. We all did."

Ridge punched my shoulder lightly. "Way to kick ass and get yourself out of there."

"Thanks for coming to help."

I hadn't seen Ridge, Jack, or Cooper much at Kaleb's compound, but I knew they'd come with the enforcers. Because we were family now. My chest tightened with that same pain, the good kind.

Ridge gave me a chin lift. "We'll always have your back."

Cass sniffed as she let me go. "I'm sorry I didn't foresee it. Kaleb must have a strong shield around him."

I grimaced, my jaw going tight. "He does and they can infuse the buildings around him with that shielding power."

"Shit," Cass muttered. Her eyes narrowed on some invisible spot in the distance. "There has to be a way around that..."

Jack wrapped an arm around her, turning her towards the school. "Think about world domination while we walk or we're going to be late for class."

I turned to grab my backpack, but Anson already had it slung over his shoulder. I reached for it. "I can carry it."

He bent, giving me a quick kiss. "Let me take care of my girl."

"Our girl," Keene muttered.

"Yeah, yeah, you know what I mean."

I chuckled as we headed towards the school doors. Maybe I did need this. The piece of normality against all the crazy. A few hours where the most important thing was giving each other a hard time and passing my English midterm.

Luc opened the door and held it for our group. I kissed his cheek as I passed. "Thanks."

"I'll take that payment any day."

We moved through the hallways crowded with other students hurrying to make their first classes. I felt the stares more than I saw them. I stayed focused on whatever was directly in front of me, and the guys formed a protective huddle to shield me from the worst of it.

We came to a stop outside the astronomy classroom. Cass kissed Ridge and Jack and gave me a quick hug. "See you at lunch."

Holden tipped my face up to him, searching my eyes. "You good?"

I stretched up on my tiptoes to meet his lips. "Good now."

He grinned against my mouth. "That's what I like to hear."

Keene tugged me against him and kissed me soundly. "Mind link me if you need anything."

"I'll be fine."

"Mind link me."

"Okay, okay. But no barging into my head just because you haven't heard from me in thirty minutes."

He chuckled and released me. "I'll try."

I rolled my eyes and followed Jack and Ridge into the classroom, Luc and Anson trailing behind.

As I headed to my seat in the back corner, a figure stepped into my path. Sadie glared daggers at me. "You think you can get me in trouble and then just hide?"

"I didn't get you in trouble and I'm sure as hell not hiding from you."

Her eyes flashed. "You got me suspended."

I had no idea what she was talking about. "Did you take a hit to the head?"

Anson chuckled, pressing himself to my back. "You missed the news, Ro. The cops found Sadie's prints on the Taser in your locker. She got suspended for a week and isn't allowed to go to winter formal."

The laugh burst out of me. Sadie probably didn't give a damn about being suspended, but missing winter formal would be a fate worse than death. I grinned at her. "Sucks when being a jealous bitch comes back to bite you."

Her face turned a shade of red rarely seen on the human form. "You're going to pay for this."

Anson let out a low growl that had Sadie stumbling back a few steps. "Stay away from Rowan."

"Freaks," she muttered and hurried to her seat.

I tipped my head back so I could see Anson's face. "Have I ever told you how sexy your growl is?"

He let a soft one slip from his lips.

"Not fair. We're in school."

A grin stretched across Anson's face. "I'll growl at you as soon as we're home."

I stretched up to give him a quick kiss. "I'm going to hold you to that."

CHAPTER TWENTY

HOLDEN'S FINGERS DUG INTO MY SHOULDERS AS WE drove up the gravel road towards the lodge. His thumbs worked at the muscles that had turned to stone in the past few hours. "I think you might've overdone it on the weights this morning."

I was going to be paying for it tomorrow, but I didn't have much of a choice. "I'll sit in the hot tub after I work on my gift this afternoon."

Mason had told us he would be putting in some calls to people who had energy benders in their family lines, hoping they might have some information to help us. I thought about the other members of the Quad, how much information they likely had on the subject, then immediately shut the idea down. They had continued to refuse to believe Kaleb was behind the attack on me, even though he'd apparently gone into hiding.

Anson came to a stop in front of the lodge, and we piled out of the vehicle as the front door opened and Mason appeared. "We need to talk."

My stomach dropped at the lines of tension bracketing his

mouth. The guys moved in around me as Vaughn appeared in the doorway. His face was a blank mask, but I could see the hints of concern in those ice-blue eyes.

No one said a word as we filed into the lodge. It was quiet. Too quiet. Especially for the hours after school. Kids were usually coming through to get an after-school snack and holed up at tables to study. The only other person present in the space now was our head enforcer, Mac. He dipped his chin in greeting, but there was no warmth in his gaze.

I wanted to move to Vaughn, to wrap my arms around him, but the edge in his demeanor told me that contact wouldn't be welcomed. The knowledge twisted something inside me, and my wolf made a keening noise in my head. She didn't understand our mate's need to hold himself back from us.

I did my best to soothe her as I sat on the sectional. Luc must've sensed my unease because he took my hand, letting a trickle of that warm, calming energy flow into me. I leaned into him in thanks.

Holden took my other side, Anson and Keene flanking us. Vaughn stayed standing, moving behind the couch. It was his perpetual position, as if he needed to be ready for an attack at all times.

I looked up, meeting Mason's gaze. "What happened?"

"There was an attack on a smaller pack last night. North of here, just over the Canadian border. Two gifted females were taken and most of the pack slaughtered."

My stomach twisted and cramped. "Kaleb?"

A muscle along Mason's jaw ticked. "The attack was done by rogues."

The word triggered a series of memories in my mind. Tidbits of information that the guys had shared about the attack on their own pack nine years ago. I swallowed, trying to clear the dryness in my throat. "Are attacks by rogues common?"

"No," Vaughn growled behind me.

Mason scrubbed a hand over his jaw. "Rogues are often hired for less than savory jobs. Things that could get you brought before the Quad. They exist on the fringes of our society and they like it that way. But it's rare for a large group to be organized in this way."

"Was it a large group that attacked Ridgewood?"

The group was silent. I glanced at Keene. There was so much pain in his gaze, it clawed at my heart. No, I could feel it. The hurt, the loss, the grief. I could feel Vaughn's rage pulsing off him in waves. And Holden? There was so much guilt swirling around in him, I could drown in it.

I grabbed his hand, squeezing hard. "It wasn't your fault."

He stared at the floor. "I should've protected her."

"You were nine years old."

I could picture little Holden losing himself in grief and guilt for the mother he'd loved so much.

"She's right," Mason said, voice hoarse. "I shouldn't have taken so many wolves with me to the conference. I left us unprepared—"

"It's none of your faults," I said, cutting him off. "The only people responsible are the ones who were involved in the attack. Did you ever find any of them?"

Mason's jaw locked so hard, it looked as if it would crack.

It was Mac who spoke. "We tracked down two of the

attackers. They never broke. Never said why they'd come. Never told us who had hired them."

Mason stared out the back windows. "But I can't help but wonder if it's been Kaleb pulling these strings all along."

Nausea swept through me, swift and strong. "Why?"

"The rogues tortured Vaughn for the locations of our shelters. They asked him where the alpha's son was."

Holden stiffened next to me and I gripped his hand tighter.

Mason shifted his gaze to his son. "You were already showing signs of dominance and my gift was no secret. It's possible he wanted to take you, to turn you to his side."

"I would've taken death first," Holden growled.

Each revelation, each word ripped at another piece of my soul. How had I come from a man who had wrought this level of pain? The agony bled into me through my bond connections. Grief, anger, guilt. It was almost too much for me to take.

Luc pinched the bridge of his nose, and I knew it was attacking him tenfold.

Mason's hands clenched into fists, knuckles bleaching white. "But he didn't succeed. He didn't get you, and after that attack, our security measures were heightened. Since the two rogues attacked Vaughn and Rowan, they've been increased even more. Kaleb won't succeed."

But he'd already stolen so much from the Ridgewood pack. Keene and Vaughn's parents. Holden's mom. Countless other family members and loved ones. And he'd kidnapped two girls from their home last night. He might not have physically been there, but he was the puppet master pulling all the strings.

How could the people in this room even look at me knowing the carnage my father had left in his wake? How could they love me when his blood flowed through my veins?

The walls closed in around me and my lungs constricted. I couldn't get air in. My hands began to tingle as I pushed shakily to my feet. All I knew was that I needed out. So I simply ran.

CHAPTER TWENTY-ONE

COOL AIR SLAPPED AT MY FACE AS I PUSHED MY MUSCLES harder. But it wasn't enough. With my shifter heat, there wasn't a bite to the air that I needed right now. Something to shock me back into breathing again.

My lungs burned and the tingling sensation spread up my arms. I bent over, gasping as my fingers curled in on themselves. There was no air. My legs wouldn't hold any longer and I crumpled to my knees.

Hands grasped my shoulders. "Just breathe," Luc soothed.

Seconds later, the worst of my panic was being pulled away. But I didn't deserve that. I should've stopped Kaleb. Ended him when I'd had the chance. Instead, I'd been terrified of what I was capable of. I shoved at Luc's hands. "Don't."

Hurt flashed across his face. "Rowan."

"I don't deserve it." Tears streamed down my face as I looked up at Luc. "I could've stopped him. Could've prevented those girls from being taken. Now they're living the worst kind of torture. Worse, their bonds might've been killed. Their families."

The panic dug its claws deeper, setting my lungs on fire. Luc sank to the ground in front of me, his hands cupping my face. "This isn't your fault. You aren't your father's keeper."

"I should've stopped him. I could've. I was too scared."

Luc hauled me into his arms, cradling me to his chest. "You're allowed to hesitate before you take a life, to take a breath before considering ending your father."

"Those girls. They're in hell because of me."

Luc held me tighter against him. "Because of Kaleb. What did you just say in the lodge? That the attack wasn't any of our faults. That it was on the rogues and the ones ordering the attack. The same is true about this."

A sob tore free from my chest. "How will they be able to look at me again? My father is responsible for all that pain. For Keene and Vaughn's parents. For Holden's mother. The reason why Vaughn is so broken."

Each word carved itself into my soul, their pain becoming my own.

Luc brushed the hair away from my face. "They love you. None of them holds you responsible just because Kaleb contributed to your DNA. You are your own person, Rowan. And that person is everything we could've ever dreamed of. Strong enough to stand up to five intense personalities, kind enough to meet us all where we are, clever enough to bring us together. You're a miracle."

I let out a shuddering breath, a few more tears falling free. Luc swept them away with his thumbs. "I'm an empath, remember? I would know if they were angry at you. All they are is worried."

The worst of my anxiety slipped away. Not because of Luc's gifts but because of his words. The power of being an empath had carved itself into him in every way. He could heal without using magic at all.

I leaned into him, my lips a breath away from his. "I love you."

"So much it feels like it claws at my insides."

My mouth pulled down.

Luc ran a finger across my bottom lip. "Why are you frowning?"

"That doesn't sound altogether pleasant."

He chuckled. "It's the ferocity of what I feel for you. I wouldn't have it any other way."

Something in me melted at that. I ran my hands along the buzzed sides of his head and then sank my fingers into his longer hair. My mouth found his, easing into the kiss. It was comfort that quickly turned into something else entirely.

Heat licked up my spine as Luc's tongue stroked mine, bringing with it a hunger that had me fisting his shirt. I shifted so that I was straddling him, his length pressing against my core. My hips moved of their own volition, seeking contact and pressure, more of Luc.

As I arched into him, he growled into my mouth. In a flash, he was on his feet carrying me farther into the woods.

"Where are you—"

My words cut off as I caught sight of the same storage shed where we'd cemented our bond weeks ago. It felt like a lifetime had passed in those weeks. And Luc felt like he was entirely mine.

He pulled open the door with enough force to send it slamming against the side of the building. As soon as it swung back, closing behind us, Luc was tugging at my clothes. My calm and collected Luc had a feral edge to him now. My shirt was tugged free, and his fingers were on the button of my jeans before pushing them to the floor.

My hands went to his tee, awkwardly tugging it over his head, not caring if it stretched or tore. All I wanted was Luc. His skin against mine. To feel all of him.

In moments, there was nothing between us. The gold in Luc's hazel eyes flashed. "You steal my breath."

His hands skimmed down the column of my neck to my breasts. One stayed there, exploring. The other dipped between my thighs, teasing and toying.

My head fell back, a pant escaping my lips. My legs trembled as two fingers slipped inside me.

Luc curled those fingers as his thumb circled my clit. I struggled to stay upright.

"I can feel you."

My gaze shot to Luc, his eyes hooded and a devilish grin playing on his lips.

"I can feel every peak of sensation." His thumb pressed down on that bundle of nerves. "Every zing of pleasure."

Luc read my body before the thoughts had even entered my brain. He could play me as if I were a violin and he a master musician.

But right now what I wanted was Luc. All of him. "Make me yours," I whispered.

His eyes flared. A second later, I was on my back on a chaise with Luc hovering over me. My legs wrapped around his waist, his tip bumping against my entrance. His lips met mine in the most tender of kisses. "Love you, Rowan."

Then he was sliding inside, and I arched up to meet him. Our bodies communicated without words. The connection of empath to bond mate was one where they weren't needed.

We spoke in strokes and caresses, building a tempo that was ours alone. My fingers curled into Luc's shoulders as he drove deeper. Each thrust imprinting himself on me in a way I knew would never leave. I didn't want it to.

I wanted the world to know I was his and he was mine.

I must've let that thought pass to him because Luc's hold on me tightened. His thrusts grew desperate and frenzied. My nails dug into his back as he took, as he did what I asked and made me his.

My mouth fell open in a silent gasp as my walls clamped down around Luc. My body grabbed hold with everything I had. We came apart together, with the knowledge we were forever bound.

CHAPTER TWENTY-TWO

L UC PULLED TO A STOP IN FRONT OF OUR HOUSE. I DIDN'T make a move to climb out of the SUV he'd borrowed from the lodge. Instead, my fingers tapped in a rapid rhythm on my knees.

He leaned over, tangling his fingers in my hair and tipping my mouth to his. "They aren't angry with you."

I believed Luc. But that didn't mean the guilt wasn't still eating away at me.

He released my seat belt. "Come on."

I opened my door and slid out of the vehicle, moving at a snail's pace. Luc rounded the SUV and took my hand in his. He didn't release any of that calming energy into me, but I was reassured simply by his touch.

We strode up the path to the house and Luc opened the door, holding it for me. I stepped inside, hovering in the entryway. For the first time, I felt as if this place wasn't mine. That I was an interloper in a world where I wasn't welcome.

Low voices drifted from the living room and Luc nudged me

in that direction. We wound our way there, coming to a stop as four sets of eyes lifted at our arrival.

I gripped my hands in front of me, squeezing my fingers tight. There were a variety of reactions to my presence. Keene and Anson looked worried. Vaughn angry. And Holden I couldn't read at all.

"Are you okay?" Anson asked.

I nodded, not saying a word.

"She's worried people will blame her for her father's actions. That we won't look at her the same," Luc said.

I sent a glare in his direction.

Holden's mouth slackened. "Ro, you have nothing to do with your father. You didn't even know who he was for most of your life."

"He's still my blood." The words were quiet, as though if I said them too loud, my reasoning would take root.

Keene pushed to his feet, striding towards me. "You are nothing like *him*."

"I might be capable of the things he is."

"Never." Keene cupped my face, bending down so that he was eye level with me. "There is no cruelty in you." His thumbs brushed across my cheeks. "Who you're related to has nothing to do with how we see you. How much we love you."

My eyes burned, but I'd shed far too many tears over the past few days. I swallowed them down. "I'm so sorry about your parents."

A hint of pain flashed across his expression. "Me too. But that weight isn't on your shoulders."

"He's right," Vaughn said gruffly. "Don't be an idiot and take that on."

I scowled at him. "Don't call me an idiot."

"Then don't act like one."

"One of these days, I'm going to junk punch him," I muttered under my breath.

Holden chuckled as he stood from the couch. Damn that shifter hearing. He crossed to us and pulled me into a hug. "I love you, Rowan. Nothing will ever change that."

I pressed a hand to his chest, reveling in the feel of his heartbeat against my palm. Strong and steady. "I hate that the person I came from has caused you all so much pain."

"We'll stop him," Holden spat with a certainty I couldn't seem to find.

"I hope you're right." But for that to be the case, I needed to find so much more strength than I had before. I glanced out the windows. It was already dark, and I'd lost my time with Mason for training. Tomorrow, I'd have to do better.

Anson moved closer. "How about a run? I think giving our wolves time together might be a good thing."

My wolf perked up at that. She always loved being free, but her favorite thing in the world was to run with her mates. I should've gone straight to catching up on homework if I wasn't going to train, but I couldn't resist the twitch of Anson's lips and hopeful look in his eyes.

"Let's go." I looked at Vaughn. "Come with us?"

There was a moment of hesitation and then he nodded.

My wolf all but preened, taking credit for his acceptance.

Anson opened the back door and we all stepped outside. As we got undressed, I couldn't help but let my eyes wander. Each of my mates was so different, but they all pulled at me. Eyes that tugged at my soul, bodies that made me burn for them.

My shift came on easily now. A coating of my magic and tingling sensation as I turned from flesh to fur. I shook out my reddish-brown coat and took in my bond. I felt the same pull to them in this form, and I didn't hesitate.

I moved to Anson, rubbing against his black and gray coat. He nipped the side of my neck playfully. I swiped my paw across his backside and he let out a chuffing laugh.

Crossing to Luc, I nuzzled him. He lapped at my face in a sloppy kiss. I let out a low growl, wiping the slobber off on his side.

Keene moved in, pressing himself against me. His silver-gray fur shone in the moonlight. I nipped his ear in greeting.

Holden stood the largest of us all, the alpha blood in him evident. His golden coat only added to his majesty. I ached to draw him just like this.

I crouched low and then launched myself at him, and we rolled in the grass. Holden needed play more than any of the other guys, the weight of the world resting heavily on his shoulders. We rolled until he pinned me to the ground. His teeth grazed my neck and I shivered.

With one last bite, he released me, getting to his paws. I rolled to stand and caught sight of Vaughn. His black fur melded with the night, but that white patch on his chest resembling a heart was my beacon.

I prowled towards Vaughn and his ears twitched. He eyed me cautiously, bracing for I wasn't sure what. I came to a stop just inches away from him. His scent hit my nostrils and I wanted to roll around in it, to have it cling to my fur.

I moved on instinct, swiping my tongue over Vaughn's cheek.

He froze, his mouth dropping open in a comical way. I grinned and did it again.

He let out a low growl.

I lowered myself on my front paws, my tail wagging. It wouldn't hurt Vaughn to have a little play either. Maybe it would ease his perma-scowl.

I surged forward, going for another swipe of my tongue, but he batted me away. I ducked, faking him out and then bit his hind quarters, none too gently. Vaughn let out a strangled howl.

Before he could seek retaliation, I darted for the trees. In mere seconds, he was hot on my heels. Howls lit the air as my mates raced after me. I dodged rocks and leapt over downed trees.

Just as I was about to reach the creek, a large form crashed into me, sending us both flying to the ground. Vaughn and I rolled, stopping just shy of the water. Seconds later, the rest of our bond descended.

It was a pile of claws and fur. Playful nips and barking laughs. Keene pounced into the water, spraying us all.

I lost track of time under the moonlight. All that mattered was this moment with my wolves as we were always destined to be. And I would fight with everything I had to hold onto this gift.

CHAPTER TWENTY-THREE

I GRABBED A TOWEL FROM THE STACK BY THE GYM DOOR. Wiping my forehead, I took a swig of water. My heart still pounded in a quick rhythm and my muscles quivered, but in just the past two weeks, I'd gotten stronger. The weights I could lift were increasing, the runs longer. That didn't mean I could let up.

Pushing open the door, I let the cool air skate over my skin. Anson trailed behind me. "Why don't we grab something to eat at the lodge?"

"I need to work on my gift first."

His lips pressed into a firm line. "You were at it for hours last night."

So long that Keene couldn't shield anymore because he was so depleted. I'd had to restore his energy reserves, which had in turn weakened my own. We'd had no choice but to stop for the night.

"I need all the extra time I can get." Because my gift wasn't reliable. I'd found my path with energy blasts, but breaking through shields? Not so much. I didn't try to push down the frustration that bubbled up. Instead, I let it feed that pool of energy at my center. The greater the pool, the greater the chance I had to finally succeed at breaking through.

"You also need to take care of yourself," Anson grumbled.

I turned around so that I was facing him but kept walking backwards. "You're just cranky because you wanted togetherness time and that means a four a.m. wakeup call."

Anson was the only one who stuck it out every day of the week. The rest of the bond rotated in and out, or simply joined for my afternoon training sessions. Anson didn't laugh like I expected. Instead, there was a hint of anger in those green depths.

My steps slowed. "What?"

He reached out, his thumb gliding along the side of my neck. "I'm worried about you."

That frustration burned brighter. "I have to push."

"There's challenging yourself and then there's being reckless."

I stepped out of Anson's hold. "I'm not being reckless."

A muscle in his cheek ticked. "You sure about that?"

My hands fisted, nails biting into my palms. "I know how much I can handle. I don't need you doubting me. It doesn't help."

Anson's expression softened, but lines of tension still bracketed his mouth. "I don't doubt you—"

"Well, that's exactly what it sounds like."

"I don't want you to hurt yourself in the training process. That's all. You've done nothing but school or training for the past two weeks. It's okay to take a break now and then. It's good."

But every time someone suggested a movie or trip to the lake, all I could think about was those missing girls who hadn't been found. How terrified and alone they must have felt. How

107

could I joke around when they were likely being tortured at the hands of Garrison 2.0?

"It needs to be this way right now." I turned on my heel and moved towards the picnic tables where Holden and Keene were talking in hushed tones.

They looked up at our approach. The wariness that filled their expressions had me swallowing a curse. Holden held out a bottle. "Brought you a protein drink."

"Thanks." I took a swig. It tasted more like chalk than chocolate, but I swallowed it down. "Okay. I'm ready."

Keene sent a sidelong glance in Holden's direction. "What if we took this morning off—"

"I need to practice. Do you want to help me or not?" The words came out more harshly than I'd intended, but my annoyance was at a boiling point. I took a steadying breath. "Sorry. If you don't want to do these morning sessions, that's fine. But I'm going to keep working at it."

I made my way over to where we'd set up a series of dummies. Some of them were burnt to a crisp from my energy blasts, others were still in good shape. Anson and Holden had been teaching me more hand-to-hand combat. Luc worked with me on my energy blasts. Keene provided shield practice. And Vaughn...

My gaze lifted to the tree line. There he was, as if I'd conjured him with my thoughts alone. Vaughn had gone even quieter than normal. He crossed his arms over his chest, looking pissed as hell.

His contribution to my training was that stare. Even when one of the other guys would try to bring him into the conversation, he wouldn't say a word. I fought the urge to stick my tongue out at him.

Footsteps sounded behind me. "I'll help."

I turned, meeting Keene's gaze. There was defeat in it. I moved into his space, stretching up on my tiptoes and brushing my lips across his. "Thank you. I feel like I'm close. I just need a little more practice."

The doubt in his eyes hurt, but I didn't blame him for it. I hadn't once broken a shield since my captivity.

Keene took a few steps away from me and focused his vision on the ground. "Ready."

He'd found a way to shield the dummies so that I didn't have to practice trying to shoot an actual person through his shields. I focused on one of the dummies that I'd previously fried in non-shield practice. I closed my eyes and tugged on that golden pool at my center. I let it flow through me, down my arms and into my palms.

Opening my eyes, I thrust out my hands. Blasts of light shot from my palms. I thought for sure they'd be the ones to finally break through. But they bounced off the invisible force field Keene had created.

A growl of frustration bubbled out of me. "Again."

I shot blast after blast, trying every imagery technique I could think of. None of it worked. The harder I tried, the less success I found.

I let the anger fuel me and threw a blast so hard, it sent me stumbling back a few steps.

"Enough," Holden barked. "You're done for the day."

I whirled on him. "You aren't the boss of me."

"Maybe not, but I am someone who loves you and I'm not going to stand around and watch while you kill yourself."

My mouth fell open but I quickly shut it. I took stock of

myself. My energy levels were dangerously low. My muscles trembled with fatigue. Even my vision was blurry around the edges.

I'd pushed too hard. But what other choice did I have? I'd pored over every journal, tried every training technique shared in their pages. And time was running out.

Holden pulled me into his arms. Just the contact began filling my well again. The worst of the trembling in my muscles faded.

He brushed his lips across my temple. "You'll get there. But you have to give yourself time."

I looked up into his eyes. "What if it's too late?"

CHAPTER TWENTY-FOUR

"R OWAN."

I looked up from my locker at the sound of my religion teacher's voice. "Hi, Ms. Angler."

She nodded to the hulking form behind me. "Relax, Anson. She's not in trouble."

He moved to my side. "Of course not. Ro's the perfect student."

Ms. Angler shook her head, but a smile played at her lips. "I need to speak to this perfect student privately."

Anson frowned at her and opened his mouth to argue, but I patted his chest. "I'm fine. I'll meet you in the cafeteria."

"Call if you need me."

I knew he didn't mean on the phone. I opened my mind link to him. *Go. I'll tell you if she gives me detention and you can threaten to beat her up.*

A chuckling sound filled my head and he bent to give me a quick kiss. "See you in a bit."

As he left, I turned back to Ms. Angler. She watched Anson disappear in the crowd of students. "He's certainly protective."

She had no idea.

Ms. Angler shifted her focus back to me. "How are you feeling, Rowan? I know you were sick and then there was a death in your community—"

"I'm fine," I cut in. I didn't want to give her a chance to ask any questions about who had died because I wasn't sure what story Mason had given the school.

"I know you've had a lot of changes and hardship over the past year. It can be difficult to focus in those times. I get that. But I'm afraid you're in danger of failing my religion class."

My mouth fell open. I knew I hadn't done well on the past few quizzes and had missed a paper, but failing?

A scoffing laugh sounded to the left. "Figures," Sadie muttered as she glided by. "Too busy spreading her legs."

"Sadie," Ms. Angler chastised. "That language is not acceptable."

"Sorry, Ms. Angler." Sadie glared at me as if it were my fault she'd been reprimanded.

Ms. Angler ushered me into an empty classroom. "I'd like us to meet after school on Monday. We can come up with a plan to get you back on track. I don't want you to have to repeat your senior year."

I wouldn't last through another round of my senior year. "Sure. Maybe I can do some extra credit or retake some tests?"

"We'll talk about it on Monday." She patted my shoulder. "If you work hard the rest of the year, you shouldn't have any problems."

I nodded as she disappeared into the hallway. The chances of the rest of the year going smoothly were slim to none. Maybe I could get an automatic A for defeating my sociopath of a father? But I wasn't any closer to that than I was an A in religion. We still had no idea where Kaleb even was.

I lifted my backpack higher on my shoulder and headed into the hall. There were only a few stragglers left, and by the time I reached the cafeteria, most of the students were sitting at their tables. The feeling of eyes on me grated on my skin.

Finding the guys at our usual spot, I kept my focus on them as I wove through the sea of tables. Luc's eyes narrowed on me as I approached. "What happened?"

I pinched his side. "Stop mind reading. It's rude."

He nipped my shoulder as I took the seat next to him. "It's not mind reading."

"Close enough," Keene muttered.

Holden slid a bagged lunch towards me. "Tell us what Ms. Angler wanted."

I glared at Anson. "Gossip is a sin, you know?"

He popped a chip in his mouth. "They wanted to know where you were."

"So?" Holden pushed.

I pulled my sandwich from my bag and methodically unwrapped it, not meeting anyone's eyes. It was bad enough to admit this in front of my mates, but Cass, Ridge, and Jack were here too. "I'm failing religion," I mumbled.

Keene straightened. "What?"

"I haven't been doing great in religion. Ms. Angler wants to meet with me after school on Monday."

"Why didn't you say anything?" Holden asked.

I opened my bag of chips and pulled one out. I flipped it back and forth between my fingers. "I didn't know. I mean, I knew I hadn't done great on the last couple of quizzes..."

"We can study together for the next one," Cass cut in. "I'm doing pretty well in that class."

Luc knocked his shoulder against mine. "We can quiz you."

Anson waggled his eyebrows. "I'll come up with creative rewards for every question you get right."

"Gross," Cass said, making a gagging noise.

"Like you don't get up to the same thing with those two over there," Anson shot back.

Cass grinned. "Fair point."

I pinched the bridge of my nose where a headache was forming. I couldn't remember the last reading I'd completely finished for religion. I'd need to go back weeks if I wanted to do well on the midterm. Thinking of adding that to my training had my eyes burning.

I stared down at my uneaten sandwich as I fought back tears. Keene reached under the table and squeezed my knee. "Ro?"

"It's too much. I don't think I can juggle any more."

Holden's jaw tightened. "Of course you can't. You're already seconds from dropping."

Cass glared at him. "Not helping, buddy."

"She's going to hurt herself." He turned to me, anger heating those dark blue eyes. "You're falling asleep in classes, Anson told me you almost passed out in P.E. the other day, and there's no life in your eyes anymore."

It was the last one that had my throat constricting. "I'm doing the best I can."

The fight went out of Holden at that. His shoulders

slumped and he reached under the table to take my hand. "I know that. But I'm worried. We all are."

"It won't be for much longer. I'm close to breaking shields. I can feel it." It was the first time I had outright lied to Holden. And he knew it.

He dropped my hand and pushed back from the table. He didn't say a word as he walked away.

CHAPTER TWENTY-FIVE

The house was quiet. Too quiet. The guys were physically present, but emotionally? I wasn't so sure. I set down my religion textbook and stood. No one said a word as I headed for the stairs.

I made my way to our bedroom. Ducking into the closet, I quickly shed my school clothes and changed into workout shorts and a running tank. If a non-shifter saw me leaving the house like this in forty-degree weather, they'd think I had a screw loose, but my shifter heat combined with a run meant I wanted as few clothes as possible.

Slipping my feet into a pair of sneakers, I headed out of the space and came up short. Vaughn leaned against the door-jamb of the bedroom, his arms crossed over his chest. "Where are you going?"

"For a run."

This time it wasn't simply in pursuit of training goals. I needed to burn off some of the guilt eating at my insides. The weight of the quiet stares of my bond.

Vaughn grunted, his eyes narrowing.

My mouth tightened. "Use your words if you have something to say."

"Why? You wouldn't listen to me anyway."

That guilt churning inside me burned brighter. "I've done my homework, eaten—I don't think it's crazy to go for a run." I left out the fact that I'd already done ten miles that morning.

"Fine, but you're not going alone."

I didn't even bother arguing. It wouldn't have mattered if I did. But hurt dug itself deep into my muscle and sinew at the thought that none of the guys might *want* to be around me right now. And I didn't especially blame them.

When I didn't say anything, Vaughn disappeared into the room next door. I toyed with the strands on my bracelet. "Wish you were here, Lace."

My sister had always had the best advice. She could find that balance between being honest and kind. She'd kicked my ass if I needed it, but she'd also understood me better than anyone and could see things from my perspective.

I had a feeling there would be more ass kicking than anything else if she were here. But maybe she'd have been able to help me find a new path too. I would've given anything for a couple of hours with her to sort it all out.

Movement caught my attention and I looked up. Vaughn had changed into workout shorts and sneakers, but he'd forgone the T-shirt. I swallowed hard as I took in his expanse of muscle. His gaze was focused on my bracelet.

I released my hold on the strings. "You ready?"

He nodded, starting down the hall. When we reached downstairs, he called to the guys. "We're going on a run. Be back soon."

Their eyes lifted to us, but I quickly averted my gaze. I didn't want to see the looks of disapproval. Instead, I headed for the door, pulling it open and stepping into the cool evening air.

I pulled the smell of pine into my lungs and the other scents that had come to mean home. A pang of longing lit along my sternum. A grief at the disconnect I was feeling with my bond.

I picked up a jog, not waiting for Vaughn. The urge to move was too strong. I forced myself to keep my pace easy until my muscles warmed.

Footsteps sounded behind me, but Vaughn made no effort to join me. He was more bodyguard than mate.

The burn in my chest intensified. I increased my speed, testing my muscles. They seemed loose enough. I pushed myself harder, welcoming a different kind of burn. The kind that said I was alive and fighting.

I followed the dirt road towards the mountains, trying my best to ignore the fact that Vaughn was behind me. Memories of the past few weeks dogged me. Garrison and his torture. Kaleb's taunts. The hurt on Holden's face today.

I picked up my pace, searching for those moments of blissful nothingness when I was pushing myself to the edge. That place where there was no space for memories or thoughts of any kind. Where it was only you and the path beneath your feet.

The road gave way to a path. Branches of overgrown brush and trees slapped at my exposed skin. I welcomed any hint of pain. It was more distraction that I desperately needed.

The path turned into a steep incline, and I attacked it with everything I had in me. My rage at Kaleb. My pain and grief. My frustration and impotence.

My legs shook as I crested the last of the hill. I normally would've loved seeing the meadow that greeted me, but instead,

I struggled to stay upright. I tried to stiffen my legs, to command them to stand strong, but they wouldn't obey.

Seconds later, they gave way, sending me crashing to the ground. A thick blanket of grass cushioned my fall, but the drop still jarred my spine. My chest heaved as I struggled to get my breathing under control.

Vaughn slowed to a stop in front of me but made no move to help. "Are you done?"

I blinked up at him. "Excuse me?"

"Are. You. Done?"

I struggled to my feet, my legs still shaking with a vengeance. "No. I'm not done. I won't be done until my father is in a shifter prison or six feet under."

"Foolish," Vaughn spat.

My hands fisted at my sides as my whole body trembled. "I'm the only one who can stop him. Me. I let him get away once. It won't happen again. I have to be ready. I have to stop him."

My voice cracked and I hated the weakness in the sound. "I'll do anything." My fingernails dug into my palms, piercing the skin. "Anything." Vaughn gripped my wrists, stilling my motions. "I have to stop him."

Vaughn pulled me into his arms, holding me tight.

It was the contact with him, the one who rarely gave freely, that broke me. It splintered my tenuous hold on the world around me. And I was simply falling.

CHAPTER TWENTY-SIX

VAUGHN HELD ON AS I LET THE SOBS FREE. IT DIDN'T matter how much I tried to shove them down, how ashamed I was for falling to pieces yet again, they came anyway. Every time I thought I had gotten a handle on things, something else landed on my shoulders.

Rough hands gripped me as I cried. They held firm as I fell apart. He whispered things I couldn't make out against my hair. Nonsensical mutterings that soothed.

Then Vaughn started to rock back and forth. This glimpse of gentleness and care only made me cry harder.

"Y-you don't even like me."

The words came out garbled, but Vaughn stilled. "Don't be dumb."

That sounded a little more like Vaughn.

He sighed, his fingers tangling in my hair as he stroked. "I thought we were past that."

"You've barely talked to me for weeks. You just glare. You won't…" I let my words trail off.

"You won't let me close."

Yet here I was in Vaughn's arms. Every time I truly needed him, he was there. But I wanted him in the in-between moments too.

"I could hurt you."

It was the same refrain that played over and over again. Excuse after excuse. I shoved at Vaughn, wriggling free from his arms.

His jaw dropped. "Rowan."

"I'm so sick of your excuses." I shoved at his chest. "You aren't going to hurt me. You aren't going to hurt our bond mates."

Vaughn's nostrils flared as he prowled towards me. "You don't know that."

I gave him another shove. "I do. I know it with everything I am. But you're still acting like a coward."

"What did you say?" he growled.

It was probably the worst thing I could've said to Vaughn. It challenged everything that was so important to him. I should've been frightened of the rage pouring off him in waves, but I would never be scared of Vaughn.

"You are the bravest person I know when it comes to protecting others, but in the rest of your life? You're a fucking coward."

Vaughn launched himself at me. One moment, I was standing in the cool night air, and the next, I was engulfed in Vaughn's heat. His mouth met mine in an angry kiss. One arm held me tight against him, while the other tangled in my hair.

He tugged on the strands, demanding better access to my lips. He took and took, nipping and stroking.

And then I was in the air, legs wrapping around Vaughn's waist. His hard length pressed against my core, making me shudder, but I didn't take my mouth from his for a moment. I didn't want to chance losing this.

The rough pads of Vaughn's fingers slid beneath my tank top, sending delicious shivers skating over my skin. His hips ground into me and sparks of light danced behind my eyelids.

"Vaughn." His name was a pleading prayer, hushed syllables from my mouth to his.

It broke the last of Vaughn's reserve. He held me up with one hand under my ass, while he yanked my tank top free with his other. Then his lips were on my nipple. Teeth grazing the peak.

My head fell back, my eyes closing. Everything about it was more than I could take. Vaughn's hands on me for the first time. His mouth on my skin.

Energy sparked between us. I pressed myself tighter against Vaughn, needing more.

He lowered me to the grass without losing purchase on my nipple, but the second I was on the ground, his lips were gone. His fingers latched onto the sides of my shorts as he yanked them off.

I barely had a chance to breathe before his mouth was on my clit. There were no teasing touches, no pretty words. His lips closed around that bundle of nerves and sucked deep.

I bowed off the ground as my fingers fisted in the grass around me.

Then his mouth was gone again, and all I could feel was cold air against heated flesh.

A moment later, Vaughn was back. His body hovered over mine, as my legs circled his waist. Our eyes met, a single question in his. I answered by lifting my hips to his.

It was all Vaughn needed. He slammed into me. All raw power and need.

My fingers dug into his shoulders, and I knew my nails would leave marks. I didn't care. Vaughn was mine. I wanted the whole world to know, but most of all *him*. I needed Vaughn to see that we belonged together. That I could meet him in the feralness of his heart and not tremble.

I met him thrust for thrust, my nails digging deeper. Vaughn growled, his teeth sinking into my shoulder. Marking me. Claiming me right back.

It sent a flood of adrenaline coursing through me, and I lost my hold on the world around me. I tipped over the edge into a feral sea right along with Vaughn.

Every desperate, dominant move drove me higher. I clawed myself deeper into Vaughn in every way I could imagine. I wanted my memory to live in his very marrow. I wanted no doubt that I could take him.

I arched back, taking Vaughn impossibly deeper. On a howl, he released inside me. I took all of him and knew that neither of us would be the same.

CHAPTER TWENTY-SEVEN

THOSE ROUGHENED FINGERTIPS TRAILED UP AND DOWN my spine. Each swipe sent shivers over my skin in the most pleasant of ways. Neither Vaughn nor I had said a word in the aftermath. He'd simply rolled to his back and hauled me on top of him. So typical Vaughn.

Even though a million different things swam through my mind, I stayed quiet. I didn't want to break the spell. So scared that he would pull away again.

I wouldn't be able to take it. Not when I knew what it was to be with Vaughn. To be completely his. I couldn't go back.

Vaughn's fingers slowed their perusal of my skin. "Did I hurt you?"

My muscles tensed. That was why he'd been silent? Because he was worried he'd hurt me?

"Did I seem like you hurt me?"

Vaughn tipped my head to the side so that he could meet my gaze. "I lost myself in the moment. I could've missed—"

I cut him off with a kiss, then let my forehead drop to his, resting there. "You didn't hurt me. The only time you hurt me is when you stay away. When you put up walls and try to keep me out."

"I don't know why I ever tried, you just bulldoze them down."

I grinned against his lips. "I'm going to take that as a compliment."

He chuckled. "Stubborn."

"Bossy."

Vaughn took my mouth in a kiss. This one was gentler, deeper. It reached down to my very soul. "I love you, Ro. So much it scares the hell out of me. If I lost you…"

Those words. Ones I thought I might never get from Vaughn. They were everything. My hand trembled as I brought it to his face. "You're not going to lose me. I'm going to fight."

"*We're* going to fight. What have we learned time and again?"

"We're stronger together."

Vaughn continued his strokes on my back. "It's not only on your shoulders to deal with Kaleb."

And I'd been locking them out of that quest in so many ways. I asked them to help me train, but I had been taking on the weight of it alone. I swallowed against the burn in my throat. I thought of how it felt when Vaughn pushed me away. I'd been doing the same thing to them.

"I'm sorry," I whispered. "I don't want division and separation. Not from you or from me."

Those ice-blue eyes flashed. "I was trying to protect you."

"That may be true, but it only hurt me."

Vaughn pressed his lips to my forehead. "I'm sorry. That's the last thing I want."

"Trust yourself." I pressed my palm to his chest. "I do. Our bond does. No one thinks you'll hurt us."

"Trust takes time."

My fingers instinctively wrapped around his biceps. "Don't shut me out. I won't be able to handle it if you walk away again."

"I'm not going anywhere. I'm too selfish. I want you with me. Need to feel your skin, inhale your scent."

I shivered against him.

Vaughn groaned. "If you keep doing that, I'll take you again and you have to be sore."

I was tender but in a way I loved. The memory of today embedded into my skin.

"Let's go before you have me making more reckless decisions."

I chuckled and rolled off him, searching for my tank and shorts. We dressed quickly and started back to the house. There was no running. Just a walk through the forest with my mate. It almost seemed normal.

"What's your favorite kind of cookie?"

Vaughn lifted a brow. "My favorite cookie?"

I nodded. "You and I never have normal conversations. I want to know the everyday stuff."

"Those chocolate crinkle ones."

"The ones with the powdered sugar on the outside?"

"Yeah." He held a branch back so it wouldn't hit me. "My mom used to make them. I haven't had them in forever."

My chest constricted, and I made a vow then and there to make those cookies for him as often as possible.

"What about you?"

Vaughn appeared almost uncomfortable asking the question. He had become so used to a life of isolation, he wasn't used to making conversation. But his attempt was adorable.

"I'm a classic girl. Give me chocolate chip all the way."

"I like chocolate chip."

His tone was defensive. As if he were worried if our cookie preferences differed, we could no longer be mates. I stifled my laugh. "What about favorite movie?"

Vaughn exited the path onto the dirt road that would take us home. "I don't really watch movies."

My steps faltered. "You don't watch movies?"

He shrugged. "Not really my thing."

"What is your thing? Wrestling alligators with your bare hands for fun?"

A laugh escaped Vaughn, and the sound was the best thing I'd ever heard. It skated over my skin, leaving goose bumps in its wake. All I wanted was to hear that sound every day for the rest of my life.

"What movie do you think I *need* to watch?"

I forced my feet to start walking again. "*A Walk to Remember.*"

Vaughn sent a sidelong look my way. "What's that about?"

"A reformed bad boy and true love."

His steps slowed. "Wait. Lily watched that last year in the lodge. She was a sobbing mess. Doesn't the girl die in the end?"

I couldn't hold in my laughter. "Sometimes a tearjerker is a good thing."

"You were going to make me watch some depressing ass movie as payback, weren't you?"

My lips twitched. "Maybe."

Vaughn dove for me, lifting me over his shoulder and carrying me towards the house. "You're gonna pay for that."

"I could've said *Beaches*. That's even more depressing. Or *The Notebook*. You would've been a blubbering mess."

Vaughn's free hand came down hard on my butt.

"Hey!" I screeched as he opened the door.

I tried to wiggle off his shoulder, but Vaughn just smacked me again and carried me towards the living room. Instead of wiggling further, I reached down and pinched his ass. Hard.

The sound that escaped Vaughn's mouth was so high-pitched, it had all the other guys' heads snapping up.

Anson's brow arched. "Anything going on you want to share with the class?"

Luc's nostrils flared, and I knew he scented sex on the air. He grinned. "Good *run?*"

Keene smacked him with a pillow. But he couldn't help looking in our direction. And damn, there was so much hope in his eyes. "You guys okay?"

"I would be if this bossy behemoth would put me down."

A second later, I was sailing through the air. I landed with an oomph on the sectional.

"Rude," I huffed.

Vaughn grinned. He freaking *grinned.* The effect was so devastating, my thighs clenched. I mentally ordered myself to get a grip.

I pushed up to sitting. Everyone was smiling. Everyone except Holden. There was still hurt lacing his expression.

Guilt gnawed at me, fear hot on its heels. For the first time, I worried if I'd pushed Holden too far. Panic raced through me that maybe I'd broken something I couldn't put back together.

CHAPTER TWENTY-EIGHT

I STRAIGHTENED TO SITTING POSITION ON THE COUCH. I didn't give myself a chance to let the fear dig its claws into me. I went straight to Holden.

My hands rested on his knees as I lowered myself to the floor in front of his chair. I looked up into those dark blue eyes. It wasn't the hint of anger in them that killed me, it was the hurt.

"I'm so sorry." I didn't look away as I spoke the words. "I lied. I'm not close to a breakthrough of any kind. I have no idea what it's going to take to get there, and I'm terrified because time is running out. There's so much on my shoulders and I'm exhausted."

The fight went out of Holden, the tension in his muscles easing. His hand snaked out, gliding along my jaw and then tangling in my hair. "It might not be as heavy of a burden if you let us carry it with you."

My eyes darted to Vaughn, who stood with his arms crossed, watching us. "Someone else might have made a similar point."

"For the first time, I'm going to say that Vaughn is right," Holden muttered.

The corner of Vaughn's mouth kicked up.

These hints of smiles from Vaughn were going to be the death of me. I forced my focus away from him and back to Holden. "I love you. I'm sorry I've been pushing you out. It was wrong and it's been too damn lonely."

Holden leaned down and took my mouth in a slow kiss. "I love you too. That will never change. But don't pull that shit again. It hurts too much."

I gripped his knees tighter. "I won't. I promise. We're a team. I'm not exactly sure how that'll work when it comes to my gift or defeating Kaleb but—"

"We'll figure it out," Holden said, squeezing my neck.

God, I wanted to believe that. I wanted to hold so tightly to that glimmer of hope in my chest.

"But to do that, you need to take care of yourself. We all do."

I knew he was right. I'd felt myself crossing over a dangerous line the past few days. But I couldn't see any other way to a solution.

Luc moved in, lowering himself to the floor next to me. "Sometimes if you're pushing too hard, you can't find the right answers." His fingers stroked over my cheek. "Let your brain and body rest this weekend. It might be just what you need."

Everything in me fought against it, but still, I agreed. "Okay."

I could feel the intensity in the room release at my single word. A little more guilt made a home inside me. I'd put them through too much over the past few weeks. "How about a cookout tomorrow? We could invite Mason, Cass and the guys, and Crispin?"

Keene's mouth curved into a smile. "I think that's a great idea."

Vaughn grunted.

Anson clapped him on the shoulder. "Don't worry, you just have to people for a few hours."

I couldn't hold in my laughter as I pushed to my feet. "I need to shower."

Holden stood instantly, lifting me into his arms. "I'm partial to showers with you."

"Hey, I want in," Anson whined.

Keene was hot on our heels. "You're not leaving me out."

"I knew there was a reason we made that shower the size we did," Luc said as we hit the stairs.

Even Vaughn followed.

As we all stepped under the spray, it wasn't about the feral passion that I often felt with my mates. It was more tender. Slow kisses and lingering touches. It was about reconnecting and building our connection back up.

It was everything we needed right now. As we got out, Holden wrapped a towel around me, kissing my nose. "Love you, Ro."

A peace slid over me. "Love you too."

Anson covered my head with another towel. "Don't want you catching a cold."

I grabbed the towel now covering my eyes and twisted it between my hands. As Anson turned to head into the bedroom, I let one end fly. It cracked right across his low back and the towel around his hips fell.

He let loose what could only be described as a girly shriek and whirled on me. His hands covered manly bits. "Rowan Caldwell."

I grinned. "Modest all of a sudden?"

131

If there was one thing Anson wasn't shy about, it was his cock.

"This kind of behavior is unacceptable."

I couldn't hold in my laughter. But soon it was me shrieking as Anson lifted me over his shoulder. He carried me into the bedroom and then I was flying through the air.

I landed on the bed with a grunt. "What is with you people and tossing me around like a sack of potatoes?"

Luc sent me a grin. "Do people throw sacks of potatoes often? I never understood that saying."

"The saying isn't the point." I struggled to sit up, my hands going to my towel that had come loose. "It's not nice to throw people around."

"It's not nice to abuse people with towels either," Anson said, as he pulled on a pair of pajama bottoms.

Holden tossed me a pair of sleep shorts and a tank. "She's keeping you in line. Someone has to."

"Hey, I've been a responsible member of the team lately."

Holden snorted.

Vaughn crossed to the bed, now in a pair of sweats. Instead of going to the end of the mattress, he lowered himself to the spot next to me. He lifted a towel and wrapped it around my head. "He was right about you catching a cold."

My breath hitched as Vaughn tucked one end of the fabric in to hold everything in place. "I thought shifters didn't get sick."

Keene crawled into bed on the other side of me. "We don't get cancer or diseases like that, but we can get infections or things like pneumonia."

"So much for being invincible."

The rest of the guys climbed into bed, arranging themselves

around me. Tonight, it was Anson I was tied to in an effort to all stay connected and fight off the dreams.

I lifted my gaze to Vaughn's. "I'm glad you're here." The first time he'd properly joined us in bed. Something about it made everything feel right with the world.

"Me too." He pressed a soft kiss to my lips. "Love you."

I'd never tire of hearing those words. I'd never take them for granted. I wrapped the syllables around me as my eyes fell closed, holding tight and refusing to let go.

CHAPTER TWENTY-NINE

WATER DRIPPED IN A STEADY BEAT, ECHOING OFF THE walls.

"Wake up, Rowan."

That voice. My entire body locked as my eyes flew open.

Kaleb's angry stare greeted me. "You think you can escape me? That you can just go on about your pathetic little life?"

I scrambled up from the cot. I was back in that awful place. The one I swore I'd never return to.

Kaleb was in the cell with me now, his hands clenched at his sides. He wasn't quite as put together as he normally was. His shirt was misbuttoned and his hair was disheveled. But nothing about that dulled the rage simmering in his eyes.

I swallowed hard. The guys would wake me up. As soon as they realized what was happening, I'd be out of here.

"Nothing to say for yourself?" Kaleb prodded.

"If my life is so pathetic, then you should have no problem leaving me alone."

One of Kaleb's knuckles made an audible crack. "You're my

daughter. You will live up to your capabilities instead of squandering them with mates who aren't worthy of you."

The only reason he thought the guys were unworthy of me was because he couldn't control them. But I kept my mouth shut about that opinion. "And who would be worthy of me?"

Kaleb stilled, his gaze assessing. "I have several candidates ready for consideration. One can control electricity. I think that would be an interesting pairing, given your gift."

I fought the urge to shudder. The idea of bonding with anyone other than my five mates made me physically ill.

"Sever your bond and you'll have all the opportunities in the world."

"I can't." It was more than that. It would kill me. I might still be here physically, but my soul would never be the same.

Kaleb prowled towards me. "You can and you will."

"Why?"

That was the simple question I couldn't figure out. Yes, there was that stupid prophecy Kaleb had received from a seer. But that same vision had said I was a risk to him. Why reveal himself to me? His plans would've continued unhindered if he hadn't.

Kaleb's eyes shifted the slightest amount. There was something there. Something we didn't know about.

"What do you want from me?"

A muscle along his jaw ticked wildly. "You're my daughter. You're meant to rule at my side."

"Your idea of father-daughter bonding is a friendly torture session, so I doubt that's it."

Kaleb grinned at me, but it was all teeth. "We can do another round of that if you'd like."

"I think I'll pass, Daddio."

135

He scoffed. "Fine. You're right. I'd rather kill you and be done with it."

The casual way he tossed those words out was like he was talking about throwing away a pair of shoes he'd decided didn't fit his style. But I guess that truly was all I was to him. An easily replaceable accessory.

"Then why aren't you doing it?"

It was a dangerous challenge, but Kaleb hadn't killed me yet. There had to be a reason.

The fluttering of that muscle in his jaw was back. "There are those who don't support a monarchy."

I snorted. No shit, Sherlock. "People aren't usually fans of having their wills subjugated." And I had to hope that his reticence of those who would be against him meant they were a formidable force. But they also wouldn't be prepared because no one believed Kaleb was capable of this.

"I know what's best for them."

"What about the girls you kidnapped? Or the shifters you slaughtered to take them? Is that what was best for them?" Rage pumped hot and fast through my veins.

A hint of surprise flickered across Kaleb's expression. He hadn't realized I'd known what he'd done. "It was necessary. Being a ruler means making hard decisions."

"Except you aren't a ruler." No one had put him in a position of power. No one except himself and his delusions of grandeur.

"It's my destiny," he growled.

"If it was your destiny, then you wouldn't have to kill people to get there."

"Are you sure about that, little energy bender? You killed a man right over there in a fight to claim your destiny."

My palms dampened and my stomach roiled. I could still see the shifter's wide eyes as he fell. The blank stare that never blinked again. "I was defending myself."

"And so am I. I'm defending my way of life. Defending our gifts. If we continue on this current path, we will lose all our power."

He truly believed that. But I was starting to wonder if the power had fled because there were those in our midst who were so hungry for it, who would do anything to take more *instead of doing good with it. The thought had me considering my own issues with my gift. I'd been pushing so hard, trying to force it, maybe that was why it was escaping me. I was too focused on the power and not the good I was trying to achieve with it.*

"You like your power, don't you, Rowan?" *Kaleb pushed.*

"Sometimes." *It was the truth. There were times it terrified me, other times it held me in rapt awe.* "But I'd never hurt people to keep it, especially those who've done nothing to deserve it."

"Weak," *he spat.* "I can't believe I spawned such a coward for a daughter."

I stiffened, my hands clenching at my sides. "The only coward here is you. The one who steals others' powers and pretends they're his own. But they aren't. Just because you've forced them into your army doesn't mean you own their gifts. It doesn't make you strong. It makes you the weakest of them all."

"You think I'm weak?" *Kaleb's voice grew tighter with each word.*

He lifted his hands and wind spun around us. This wasn't a gentle breeze like he'd used in Holden's room to disguise our conversation. This was akin to a hurricane.

My hair whirled around me, whipping across my face.

"*I'll show you* weak. *And you'll beg me for mercy.*"

A bolt of lightning shot out of his fingertips.

I tried to throw myself out of its path, but the wind held me in place. It hurtled towards me and there wasn't a thing I could do about it. Then there was nothing but pain.

CHAPTER THIRTY

MY EYES FLEW OPEN AS I WRITHED IN AGONY.
"Rowan." Luc's hands were on me in a flash, pulling away the worst of the pain.

"Shit. The tie came loose in the night," Anson said, holding up the bathrobe tie. "I'm so sorry."

"Not your fault." I could barely get the words out as Luc pulled more of the pain.

A muscle in Vaughn's jaw ticked. "Where does it hurt?"

I did a quick mental survey. It ached everywhere but the worst was along my ribs. "My side."

Vaughn was instantly tugging up my tank top. Keene sucked in a sharp breath.

I looked down and stopped breathing altogether. The black mark that had appeared on my chest after my first dream had faded in a number of hours. But something told me this mark wouldn't fade as easily.

A ragged lightning bolt cascaded down my ribs. I prodded gently on the skin and immediately hissed as pain rocked through me. Luc tugged at more of my hurt. I shook my head. "I'm okay. Don't wear yourself out."

Luc simply kept pulling on that thread of pain until the worst that I felt was a dull ache. I collapsed back on the pillows as the buzz of his warmth took over my body.

Keene brushed the hair out of my face. "How do you feel now?"

"Like I have a Luc high."

Normally the guys would've laughed at my quip, but I didn't even get a chuckle.

"What happened?" Holden asked quietly.

"Kaleb."

Vaughn let out a low growl.

I toyed with the hem of the comforter. "He needs me for something."

"If that's the case, then why is he trying to kill you?" Anson barked.

"I made him angry."

The room around me stilled.

Holden pinched the bridge of his nose. "Please tell me you weren't trying to get a rise out of a member of the Quad. The same person who has it in his head that he should rule over the entire shifter community."

My fingers tightened around the comforter. "I needed information."

"Did you get any?" Keene asked.

The rest of the guys glared at him. Vaughn shoved his brother's shoulder. "Don't encourage her."

"I don't want Rowan in danger any more than you do, but I

understand the need for more information. To know what we're up against."

"I don't think the rest of the Quad would go along with Kaleb."

Five sets of eyes shifted in my direction.

Holden moved so that he had a better view of me. "What makes you think that?"

"He's hesitating. There's a reason Kaleb hasn't made his big move yet. There are people that could stop him."

Luc pushed to a sitting position. "She makes a good point. Why hasn't Kaleb simply tried to take over the entire council?"

"He'd have to take out the rest of the Quad. I doubt any of them would want to bow down to him after sharing ruling power for so long. He needs brute force on his side," Vaughn said.

Keene scowled. "Or a hell of a lot of gifted shifters."

"Who put the Quad in power?" I had never thought to ask what had given these four shifters authority over us all.

"The trials," Holden explained. "Whenever a Quad member dies or steps down, the current members invite those they think worthy to participate in a series of trials to determine the most dominant shifter. There is hand-to-hand combat in wolf and human forms, testing of the shifter's gift, and a series of interviews."

"But the Quad picks the member. Not the entire shifter community?"

Holden nodded. "They have the ultimate say in it."

Everything about it was wrong. So much power held by so few. Being the strongest didn't necessarily make you the best leader. Our entire community was out of balance.

"What is it?" Keene prodded.

"It's so wrong. Everyone should have a voice in what happens in our world."

Luc ran a hand up and down my thigh in soothing strokes. "It's never been that way. It's always been the most dominant wolves that have ruled."

Maybe that was why everything was such a mess. Gifts dying out, weaker packs being attacked. We weren't valuing what was most important. How our unique makeups gave us all a role to play in our world. But those who were power-hungry would never see what each individual shifter could bring to the table. They only saw strength and weakness.

Crispin's small arms wrapped tightly around me. "You're sure you're okay?"

I hugged him back for the dozenth time that day. "I'm fine. I promise." My ribs ached something fierce but that wasn't important.

He looked up at me, worry creasing his features. "But they haven't gotten the bad guy yet."

"But we will."

"We" was the operative word in that sentence. There was no more "I" where Kaleb was concerned. I would need all the help I could get.

Sarah called for Crispin. "Let's get you some lunch."

He looked up at me, unsure.

I gave his shoulder a little squeeze. "Eat. We can go in the hot tub later or play the bag toss game."

He grinned at that. "Hot tub."

I held out a hand for a high five. "You got it."

As he headed for Sarah, my timer went off. I grabbed the pot holders and opened the oven. The scent of chocolate wafted into the air. I set the tray of cookies on the stove and picked up my spatula. One by one, I set the chocolate crinkle cookies on the cooling rack.

Footsteps sounded behind me and I looked up. Vaughn had a curious expression on his face as he peered over my shoulder. My breath caught as panic flashed through me. Maybe this was too soon. Maybe he would resent the fact that I was making cookies that his mother had once made him.

"Are those…?"

I gripped the spatula tighter. "Is that okay? I know it might be overstepping—"

Vaughn cut my words off with a scorching kiss. Energy zinged from my lips to the tips of my toes. I couldn't help leaning into him, searching for more. When he finally pulled away, I'd gone breathless.

"Does that mean it's okay I made them?"

He grinned down at me. "I love that you made them."

The number of smiles and grins I'd gotten from Vaughn in the past twenty-four hours had me feeling almost drunk. "They could taste awful. It's been a while since I've baked anything. Other than the few meals I'd mastered when trying to take care of my mom, I wasn't exactly an expert in the kitchen."

Vaughn grabbed a cookie from the cooling rack and popped it into his mouth.

"Vaughn! They're hot."

He smiled around a mouthful of cookie, then kissed me again. "They're perfect. Thank you, Rowan."

The mix of Vaughn and chocolate on my tongue was almost too much to take. "Love you."

He rested his forehead against mine. "You've given me the greatest gift."

My breath hitched. "What?"

"Hope."

CHAPTER THIRTY-ONE

CASS WRAPPED AN ARM AROUND MY WAIST AND GUIDED me out of the kitchen.

"I need to bring that second batch of cookies out to the table," I argued.

"Someone else will grab them. Luc said you haven't eaten yet."

My mouth pulled down in a frown as I searched out Luc. I caught sight of him on the back patio surrounded by the guys, Cass' mates, and the rest of our guests. His eyes locked with mine and he mouthed *eat*. I stuck my tongue out at him, then smiled.

"Aren't we going out there?"

"We can if you want, but I was hoping for a little time with my bestie."

Warmth flooded me at Cass' words. I leaned into her as we headed for the sectional in the living room. "Sorry I've been MIA so much."

Cass gave me one more squeeze before releasing me and plopping down onto the sofa. "It's fair to say you've had a lot going on."

I lowered myself to sit next to her and grabbed a chip from

the plate of food she'd obviously brought in. "Oh, you know, a few things here and there."

Cass snorted, but the amusement quickly fled her expression. "Luc said you got pulled into another nightmare last night."

"Luc is a regular Chatty Cathy today."

She shrugged. "I can be charming when I want to be. It's helpful in getting answers."

I chuckled. "I'm sure you are."

I took a bite of the burger, chewing while I thought about how to explain everything to Cass. Then I just decided to start at the beginning. I told her about the time in Kaleb's jail, how Rezah had been my lifeline. I told her about the first dream and then the second.

Talking about it helped. Letting loose everything I'd pent up over the past month.

Cass took my hand and squeezed. "I'm so sorry you had to go through all that."

"I'm okay. Really. I just have a burning desire to castrate Kaleb and send him hurtling over a cliff."

A shadow passed over Cass' eyes. "Some people have an insatiable need for power and control."

My stomach twisted at her words. "It sounds like you know that from experience."

She toyed with the edge of a throw pillow. "The pack I was in before this…the alpha and his son were obsessed with having gifted shifters in our ranks."

"Like you."

Cass nodded. "They hadn't had a seer in generations. The son, Argent, he got sort of fixated on me."

Nausea swept through me. "Cass…"

"I got away. That's what matters. But the alpha was trying to buy gifted female shifters on the black market."

I shot up straight. "Women are *sold?*"

"It's not talked about often, but it happens. Just like trafficking in the human world. Only in the shifter world, it's not just an obsession with youth and beauty—these traffickers are looking for powers too."

"The rogues?"

"Yes." Cass looked out the window. "But they've gotten more organized lately."

My hand tightened on my can of Diet Coke. "We've been wondering if Kaleb's pulling their strings."

Anger flitted across Cass' expression. "He is supposed to serve. Swore to protect us all when he took a seat on the Quad. If he's the one behind this, it's treason."

———⋖❊⋗———

Keene's arms went around me as I burrowed into his side. His lips skimmed my temple. "Good day?"

"Really good day." The words came easily. Even with learning what hardships Cass had faced and the darker parts of our world, the light had drowned that out. Playing in the hot tub with Crispin. A few competitive rounds of bean bag toss. Eating more desserts than I thought possible. Laughing as Mason told stories about the guys when they were young. It was exactly what we'd all needed.

Anson curved around my other side, kissing that spot he loved on my neck. "Love seeing you happy."

I wove my fingers through his. "I love seeing you getting trounced by Crispin in bean bag toss."

Holden barked out a laugh. "Me too. Highlight of my day."

Anson pinched my side lightly. "It's not nice to celebrate my defeats."

"It is when it's at the hand of a nine-year-old," Vaughn quipped.

Luc let out a snort. "He's got a point there."

"I think all of your assholishness means I get to sleep next to Rowan tonight."

Holden raised a brow. "How do you figure that?"

"I need the cuddles after you've all been so mean."

Everyone laughed, but I shivered. Memories from my dream last night swirled around in my mind.

Keene swept his thumb across my cheek. "Hey. You okay?"

"Just thinking about the dream."

Anson's fingers tightened around mine. "We'll be extra careful tonight."

"I know." Fear was certainly making itself at home in my chest, but it was more than that. My talk with Cass, the dream, my breakthrough with Vaughn, strands from all of them were weaving together to form a new image in my mind. "I have an idea."

A wary look filled Vaughn's face. "One that puts you at risk?"

"One that requires shield practices."

"Ro, you promised to take a break this weekend," Holden said.

"I know and I won't do it if we're not all on board. But this is different. I have an idea and it involves all of us."

The guys shared glances.

Anson squeezed my hand. "I'm in as long as you don't push things too far."

"Me too," Keene agreed.

Luc looked my way. "I'll be able to read if her levels are getting low."

I rolled my eyes. "I'll tell you if they're getting too low." I turned to Holden and Vaughn. "Please?"

Vaughn grunted. "Fine."

Holden let out a breath. "Not too much."

I locked gazes with him. "I promise. A couple of tries and that's it."

He nodded and got to his feet.

We made our way outside to the back patio.

"Where do you want to do this?" Keene asked.

"First, I need you guys."

They all looked my way, surprise evident on their faces.

"We've said time and again that we're all stronger together. I've been so focused on the prophecy saying I needed to be the one to end Kaleb, I lost sight of that. I think the only way I'm going to be able to break through his defenses is if our connection is strong."

Luc smiled as he strode towards me. His hands framed my face and he pressed his lips to mine. The kiss was all Lucas. That warm buzz of comfort and spark of sensation. His tongue stroked mine, making my belly tighten.

"Love you, Ro," he whispered against my lips.

"Love you too."

Anson moved in behind me, his lips trailing up my neck. "You've got this."

I could feel his belief in me in his words.

Keene came to my side, pressing a kiss to my temple. "I'll never be happier to have my ass kicked."

I grinned and gave him a quick kiss.

Vaughn moved in next to Keene. He leaned his forehead against mine, and I could feel the pulse of power in our connection. "We're with you."

"I know."

My eyes lifted to Holden as he completed the circle around me. "You were made for this, Ro. You just have to believe that."

I let my eyes close for a moment, as I felt the strands of energy linking us together. They were stronger than ever since Vaughn had stopped holding himself back. For the first time, our bond truly felt complete. I had to trust that these connections, this bond of destiny, would be enough.

I opened my eyes and let out a breath. "I'm ready."

Keene moved in the direction of the forest then turned to face me. Lines of concentration creased his brow. "I'm shielding this tree." He pointed to a large trunk.

I nodded and stepped forward. Every other time, I'd gone with sheer force. But not now.

I closed my eyes again and felt that golden pool of energy at my center. It was fuller than it had ever been, thanks to my mates. I inhaled deeply and opened my eyes. Lifting my hands towards the tree, I let the energy flow through me. I spurred it on with hope for justice and safety for all those I loved and shifters as a whole. I held an image of my bond mates in my mind and let the power fly.

Golden streaks of energy shot out of my palms. I held my breath as they cracked through the air. This time, instead of bouncing off the invisible force field Keene had created, they shot right through it and embedded themselves in the tree.

We all stood stunned silent. I'd done it. I'd broken through.

After weeks of pushing myself past the breaking point. Of trying all the things that never would've worked. I'd finally found the source of my true power. My mates. Our connection. There was a surge of joy, but it quickly faded. Because my success only meant one thing.

It was time to kill my father.

CHAPTER THIRTY-TWO

"**I**T FEELS WEIRD TO BE GOING TO SCHOOL TODAY," I SAID as we slid out of Anson's Range Rover.

We'd spent most of the day yesterday working on shield breaking. Now that I wasn't forcing things anymore, it didn't take nearly as much out of me. While we'd done that, Mason and Mac had focused on trying to locate Kaleb. So far there was nothing.

Holden wrapped an arm around my shoulders, tugging me to his side. "We need a bit of normal."

"Says the genius acing all his classes," I muttered.

He grinned as he kissed the top of my head. "I could tutor you…"

Keene snorted. "Doesn't sound like a whole lot of studying would be going on in those tutoring sessions."

"It's important to reward the student for her hard work," Holden shot back.

"I don't want in on the studying, but I'm there for the reward." Anson gave my ass a tap as he spoke.

I didn't hesitate in pinching his butt in return.

"Hey," he griped.

I shrugged. "Just a little reward for showing up to school."

Luc chuckled as he pulled the door open. "Let's try to get through the day without one of us ending up in detention."

I groaned. "I have that meeting with Ms. Angler after school."

Holden kneaded a knot in my shoulder as we walked down the hallway. "It'll be fine. She's not into giving riveting lectures, but she's nice. She'll try to help."

I hoped so. I did not want to repeat my senior year.

Holden gave me a quick kiss outside my astronomy classroom. "See you at lunch."

"See you," I grumbled.

He nipped my bottom lip. "Don't pout."

"Easy for you to say."

Keene tugged me from Holden's grasp. "I'll let you pout all you want. School sucks."

"I always knew you were my favorite."

"Hey," Anson chided.

I lifted a shoulder and then let it drop, a grin playing at my lips. "Guess you'll just have to try a little harder."

Anson lunged, taking my mouth in a kiss that scorched me to the spot. Students hooted and hollered in the classroom.

"Mr. Montgomery, I think that's enough. Ms. Caldwell needs her face in place to attend class."

My cheeks burned. "I'm going to kill you for that."

Anson just grinned one of those cat-got-the-canary smiles. "Worth it."

Luc shook his head. "I can see that hoping for no detention today was too lofty a goal."

153

We wound our way to our seats next to Ridge and Jack, who greeted us with chin lifts.

Sadie turned in her seat, scowling at me. That scowl melted into a look of concern when her eyes landed on Anson. "How are you, A?"

He blinked a few times. "Fine."

She scooted her desk closer. "My mom misses you. She asked me to invite you over for dinner tonight."

Was this chick for real? She was using her mom to try to get in Anson's pants?

"Can't tonight, but tell your mom I said hi."

Sadie gave an exaggerated frown. "She'll be so disappointed. How about tomorrow?"

"Can't come tomorrow or the next day either. I wouldn't go to dinner with anyone who has treated Rowan the way you have."

Warmth flooded my system at his words. I reached out and linked my fingers with his, a silent thank you for his support.

Sadie's expression darkened as she leveled me with an angry stare. "She's going to ruin your life."

"Watch your mouth," he snapped. "Having Rowan in my life is the best thing that has ever happened to me."

Sadie's jaw dropped. "You talk about her like she's your wife or something."

"She's a hell of a lot more than that, and she always will be."

I meandered down the hallway in the direction of my religion class.

"Stop dragging your feet." Holden took my hand and tugged me along. "The sooner you get in there, the sooner you'll be done."

"But if I don't go in there, I don't know how bad things really are." The words were out of my mouth before I could stop them. Even with all the terrifying things I'd faced recently, the idea of failing a class struck fear in my heart.

Holden halted his progress, moving us to the side of the hallway. His hand slid along my jaw and into my hair. "You're really worried about this, aren't you?"

I toyed with the hem of his T-shirt. "What happens if I have to repeat my senior year?"

"It won't come to that. I promise."

"How can you be so sure?"

He brushed his lips across mine. "Because you can do anything you set your mind to. You've proven that time and again."

I leaned into Holden. "You always know the right thing to say."

"Only when it's you."

I let out a shaky breath. "Okay. I'm ready to face the nightmares of high school."

Holden chuckled and led me towards the classroom. "You're a fierce warrior."

"Yeah, yeah." I stopped at the door. "Are you guys hanging around?"

"Of course. We'll be in the library doing homework. Come find us when you're done."

"See you later." I stretched up, giving him one more kiss, then stepped into the classroom.

"Oh good, Rowan. I was just going over a plan to get you back on track."

I swallowed and moved to the chair next to Ms. Angler's desk. "Thank you for doing this."

"It's not a problem. You're a bright girl, there won't be any failure on my watch."

I couldn't help but smile at that. She sounded more like a secret superhero than a teacher.

Ms. Angler slid a paper across the desk to me. "I don't think you need to cover every section of the textbook. I went over your tests and quizzes and these are the areas you need help in."

My eyes scanned the sheet. It wasn't nearly as bad as I'd been expecting. The topics on the list were ones in the latter half of chapters that I hadn't had time to read. I could make those up in a matter of weeks. "I can handle this."

"Good. Let's get a jump-start. I'll go over the most important ones with you now."

It was a shame Ms. Angler left us to our own devices for so much of class because she was a great teacher. She explained things in a way that was easy to understand and remember. We went through everything she thought I needed the most help on, and by the time we were done, I felt loads better.

She checked her watch. "It's later than I anticipated. You better get going, and I need to get to an appointment."

"Thank you so much for all of your help. I really appreciate it."

She patted my shoulder. "Anytime, Rowan."

I gathered my book and notebook and headed for the door. The main overhead lights had been turned off, so only the overnight emergency ones still glowed. It cast the hallway in an ominous glow. I picked up my pace as I hurried for my locker.

Spinning the dial in my combination, I tugged it open. As I reached for my backpack, footsteps sounded behind me. I started to turn, but before I could get a good look at whoever it was, a fist shot out, cracking across my temple. Pain bloomed and the world went sideways.

CHAPTER THIRTY-THREE

THE BLOW MADE MY BRAIN RICOCHET AROUND IN MY head. Everything went blurry with the force of it. I struggled to straighten, only to be greeted with a hard shove back into the lockers.

The face that came into view was one dripping with menace. "It's time for you to learn some manners."

I blinked a few times, bringing Chris' face into focus. *Shit.*

He charged towards me, but I darted out of his way, anger bubbling to the surface. I was so sick of people trying to use their strength to keep others down. To try to force me to go along with whatever they thought I should do.

Chris lunged and I gave a swift kick to his side. He grunted but quickly straightened. He grinned, but it was a twisted expression. "Did Anson tell you I study martial arts? Got my brown belt last week."

Double shit. I rolled to the balls of my feet as my head throbbed. My hands went up, guarding my face the way Anson and Holden had taught me.

Chris threw a palm strike at my chest. I deflected the worst of it, but he made enough contact to steal the breath from my lungs. I coughed as I straightened, and Chris laughed. He rounded with a kick that caught me in my side, but I used the opening to land a hard punch to his kidney.

He let out a string of expletives as he charged again. Chris might've had the size, but I had the speed. The combination of my small stature and shifter quickness helped me evade his next several blows.

"What the hell is wrong with you and your psycho girlfriend? Your obsession is getting a little old."

Redness crept up Chris' neck and into his face. "Don't talk about Sadie like that."

He let another palm strike fly, but I dodged it easily. His anger made him sloppy.

"I'm only calling it like I see it. She's begging Anson to come over for dinner, following me around like a rabid puppy, convincing you I'm the spawn of Satan—what would you call it?"

Chris' steps faltered for a moment. "She didn't ask Anson to come over."

God, this guy had a screw loose. That was all he picked up from what I'd said? "Ask anyone in our astronomy class. She wouldn't give it up until he said he wanted nothing to do with her. A real winner of a girlfriend you've got there."

It was the wrong thing to say. Rage blasted through Chris, propelling him forward into a roundhouse kick. I did my best to deflect, but it sent me stumbling back into the lockers, the breath knocked out of me.

Before I could right myself, Chris grabbed me by the hair,

pulling me to a standing position. "She warned me about you. How you can convince anyone of your lies."

"I'm not lying," I gritted out. "You know it."

"I know that you spread your legs to get people on your side." He moved his face in close. "Maybe it's time I see what all the fuss is about."

My stomach roiled, nausea sweeping through me. My knee came up on instinct and connected with Chris' groin in a hard blow.

He let out a strangled sound, his grip on my hair loosening. I didn't waste a second. My hand struck out in a palm strike to his nose.

Chris cried out as blood spurted. He gripped his face. "What the fuck?"

Rage coursed through me. "What the hell is wrong with you?"

He charged like a linebacker, but I simply stepped to the left. Chris managed to clip my side, but the hit wasn't hard enough to do damage.

His hands fisted at his sides. "You don't have Cass and her damn Taser now."

"I don't need it." I was done playing games. When Chris lunged for me this time, I let the energy swirling inside me rise to my fingertips. He looked confused for a moment when I didn't ready myself to fight. Instead, I simply let the power fly.

I held back on the sheer force that wanted to explode out of me. I guided it with the intention to stun, to warn, to scare. Crackles of light shot out of my palms.

Chris' eyes went wide. As the energy hit him, his entire body went into a spasm.

As soon as he hit the floor, I pulled my power back, and it came with ease. Then I simply stepped around Chris, writhing on the floor, and pulled my backpack and books out of my locker.

"Chris?" a shrill voice demanded.

I turned to Sadie, hands on hips. She didn't look all that concerned about her boyfriend, who was clearly in pain. She looked...annoyed. No, pissed.

"I told you to teach her a lesson."

I stiffened, a million thoughts running through my head. I slammed my locker and prowled towards her. "You told your boyfriend to attack me? To *rape* me?" Because that had been what was beneath his threats.

Sadie pointed her nose in the air. "You'd probably like it. You—"

I didn't give her a chance to finish. My hand shot out, making contact with her chest. Energy flew from my palm, grabbing hold of Sadie. "Doing that to another girl? That makes you lower than low. If you ever come near me again, if I ever hear of you messing with anyone else? I'll end you."

I pulled my power back with a snap, and she flew back into the lockers. As Sadie sank to the floor, eyes wide with terror, thundering footsteps sounded in the hallway.

Ro, where are you? It was Luc's panicked voice in my head. *I felt pain. Fear.*

Shit. Apparently my adrenaline had kept the worst of the emotions hidden from Luc, but now it was fading. *I'm fine. I'm by my locker.*

The footsteps intensified. Four hulking males skidded to

a stop. It must have looked ridiculous. Me with my bulging backpack. Chris groaning on the floor. Sadie shaking in fear.

Anson's chest rose and fell in ragged breaths. "What. The. Hell. Happened?"

Oh crap. Someone was going to die.

CHAPTER THIRTY-FOUR

I MOVED TO ANSON, PLACING A HAND ON HIS CHEST. HIS heart beat rapidly against my palm. I reached up, forcing his head down so that our eyes locked. "I'm okay."

"What. Happened?" he gritted out.

I swallowed hard. "These two geniuses thought it would be a brilliant idea to jump me in the hallway. But that didn't work out so well for them."

My words didn't seem to ease the tension thrumming through Anson.

Holden's eyes glowed in the low lights of the hallway. "Why didn't you mind link us?"

I stilled. Why hadn't I? There had been a few moments in the fight where I'd been truly scared, yet I hadn't reached out. "I forgot."

Holden froze, his only movement the fisting of his hands. "You forgot?"

"This whole shifter thing is new to me, remember?" I kept my voice low, knowing the guys would be able to pick up the words, but Sadie and Chris wouldn't.

Keene ran a hand through his hair. "That is something that's kind of important to remember."

"Sorry."

Luc moved to my side, his hands running over me. "You're hurting."

"Just a little."

"No, your head and your ribs are killing you." He lifted my shirt, exposing my side where a large red mark showed over the lightning bolt I'd been marked with a few days ago.

Anson's nostrils flared. "What did he do?"

"Tried to use me for martial arts practice, but he didn't succeed. I'm fine. I promise."

Anson let out a low growl.

"Hey." I lifted my hands to Anson's cheeks, ignoring the flare of pain in my side. "I really am okay. A couple of bumps and bruises. By tomorrow, it will be like none of this happened."

His head dipped and nuzzled the side of my neck. "He could've really hurt you."

"But he didn't."

"You have to call when you need us. You aren't alone anymore," Holden said.

My gaze shifted to him. I could hear the remnants of hurt in his voice. "This wasn't me trying to go it alone. I swear. Everything just happened so fast. I was at my locker and the punch came out of nowhere—"

"He punched you?"

Anson's words felt as if they rattled the walls around us.

Sadie let out a whimper and Chris scrambled to his feet. His expression was a mixture of fear and rage. "What are you? Some kind of alien?"

Despite the perilousness of the moment, I had the urge to laugh. "Yes. I'm some weird alien who can zap you onto another planet, so stay the hell away from me."

I fluttered my fingers at him and he stumbled back a step. I did laugh then.

Chris' face flamed as his gaze shot to Anson. "This is who you hang out with now? These *freaks?*"

Anson was in front of me one second and gone the next. He moved so fast, he was a blur of motion. He had Chris by the throat and slammed him up against the lockers. "You don't talk about her."

"Anson—"

Holden grabbed my arm. "He needs to do this. If Chris pushes anymore, we won't be able to stop ourselves. And Chris won't survive the repercussions."

I swallowed, trying to clear my tightening throat. I didn't want this. As vile as Chris was, I didn't want another death on my conscience. If I just would've struck out with my powers and incapacitated him instantly, we could've avoided all of this.

It was a balance, I realized. Knowing when to hold back and when to attack. Understanding exactly how much power you needed to let loose.

Holden wrapped his arms around me. "We love you, Rowan. And that means we'll do anything to protect you. Even if you don't like our methods."

"Tell me you won't utter Rowan's name again," Anson demanded.

"Fuck you, man."

Anson's hand tightened around Chris' throat. "I'm giving

you more chances than I should to get smart. Promise me you won't ever speak about Rowan again. That you'll stay far away."

"And I said *fuck you*." The words were barely audible through Chris' constricted airway.

My stomach cramped as Anson's hand tightened further.

"It's enough," I said.

"It's not enough for me," Anson growled.

In one swift move, Anson unsheathed his claws. No other part of his body transformed, just the long, vicious claws jutting out of his fingertips. Yet I could feel the dominant vibes wafting off him.

Chris paled as his jaw dropped open. "W-what?"

"You so much as breathe on Rowan and you die. This is to remind you of that fact."

Anson's claws sliced across Chris' chest.

He cried out and collapsed to the floor as Anson released him.

Anson's claws instantly retracted and he wiped the blood on his jeans. "Let's get out of here before I change my mind and end him."

Sadie's eyes jumped around the group. She opened and closed her mouth, as if she were trying to speak, but no words came out.

Anson glared in her direction. "That warning goes for you too. Stay the hell away from Rowan. From me. From all of us."

Her head bobbed up and down in a manic nod.

Anson prowled down the hallway. It was as if his wolf half still had the reins. He moved with that animal intensity, his head on a swivel, looking for any would-be assailants.

My throat burned as Holden guided me after him, Keene and Luc on either side of us.

Luc moved in closer. "You okay?"

I couldn't help but feel like all of this was my fault. Not acting fast enough with enough force. I nodded but knew it wasn't convincing. "I just want to go home."

Holden squeezed my shoulders. "That we can do."

CHAPTER THIRTY-FIVE

THE BUBBLES CONSUMED ME AS I SANK DEEPER INTO the bath. The heat of the water soothed away the worst of the aches and pains. I tipped my head back against the rim of the massive tub and closed my eyes.

The rage coursing through Anson's face flashed in my mind. My eyes flew open. So naptime wasn't a great idea right now.

A soft knock sounded on the bathroom door.

"Come in."

The door slid open quietly, and Anson stepped inside, shutting it behind him. His hair was damp from his shower. He was shirtless, only in low-slung gray sweatpants.

He crossed towards me but moved slowly. I hated the hesitancy in those steps.

Anson eyed me warily as he came to a stop near the tub.

I pulled a hand out of the bubbles and reached out to him. He took it instantly, the tension in his shoulders easing a bit. He lowered himself to the floor next to the tub and leaned in to nuzzle my neck. "Love you, Ro."

"Love you too." My voice cracked on the words.

Anson pulled back a fraction, pain in his eyes. "Did I scare you?"

"What? No." More guilt swirled as I pulled him to me. "You could never scare me. I just hated that you had to do that because I didn't act quickly enough."

Anson jerked away from me, his eyes flaring. "None of this is your fault."

I let my hand fall back into the water. "If I would've used my gift as soon as he attacked, then it wouldn't have gotten as far as it did."

Anson's thumb stroked the side of my neck. "We aren't supposed to use our gifts in public unless absolutely necessary. You were right to try to defeat him hand-to-hand first. You just should've mind linked us."

More guilt pricked at me. "I know that. I just—I—"

"You panicked, which is completely understandable."

"I didn't panic. I was focused on the problem in front of me."

A muscle in Anson's cheek ticked. "Which should never have been a problem to begin with. I'm so sorry I brought them into your life. I've been kicking myself over and over—"

"Anson." I lifted a hand to his face. "Their actions aren't on you. There's nothing you did that invited that."

He grunted.

"You sound like Vaughn. Use your words."

The corner of his mouth kicked up. "You wound me."

I shook my head but smiled. "I don't blame you for any of this. I just hate that you had to hurt someone who was your friend."

Anson's green gaze darkened as his hand tightened on the

side of the tub. "He was obviously never a true friend if this is what he does to someone I love."

Anson had a point there. I leaned into him. "I'm still sorry."

"It would've had to happen at some point. They were too fixated on you. I should've seen it sooner, taken stronger action after they put that Taser in your locker."

"You thought they'd move on, hoped they'd get over it. There's nothing wrong with that."

"There is when you get hurt in the process."

I nuzzled into Anson. My beautiful protector, who carried so much on his shoulders. "I love you."

It was all I could give him in the hopes it would soothe the worst of his ragged edges. That and all of me. I stretched up, my lips meeting his. I poured everything I had into that kiss. All the things I didn't have words for and hoped he would understand.

Anson met me stroke for stroke, our tongues dueling in a rhythm that had heat pooling low in my belly. But I needed more.

As I reached for that more, Anson pulled me from the tub. In a flash, I was wrapped in a towel and in his arms as he strode out of the bathroom.

Bedroom.

The command had been ordered from Anson, sent out to our bond. Footsteps sounded in the hall, and it was only moments before the rest of the guys charged into the room.

"What—" Keene's words were cut off as Anson pulled my towel free and laid me on the bed. He grinned. "Oh."

Then he was on the bed too, kissing the daylights out of me. Kissing each one of the guys was a different experience. They each brought me to places so unique and wonderful, it was like a new world. Keene brought a steady pressure that had me clenching my thighs together.

A hand slid between those thighs. Vaughn's callused fingers slid along my skin until they found my core. I sucked in a breath as he began to stroke.

Keene grinned against my lips. "Like that?"

I answered with another kiss. Taking more and more.

Anson's lips closed around my nipple, adding another instrument to the symphony of sensations.

"Hell," Holden muttered as he moved to the bed.

My hand went for the band of his sweats, tugging it down. My fingers closed around his shaft, stroking. He hissed out a breath and a thrill zinged through me. There was nothing better than when Holden let go.

A finger circled my clit and I knew it was Luc. The way he played my body because he knew exactly what I was feeling. He strummed that bundle of nerves, riding the waves coursing through me.

There was no greater high than the feeling of all my mates touching me. My back arched as another moan slipped free.

Vaughn muttered a curse as his finger slid inside me. "You feel like heaven."

My hips rocked as I met the thrusts of his fingers.

Luc bent his head, his tongue flicking over my clit. Sparks of light danced across my vision.

My grip on Holden tightened a fraction, and he let out a groan of pleasure. My hand worked up and down, relishing every flicker of response.

"Rowan," he growled.

I didn't let up. Instead, I found Anson too. I moved in sync as Keene's lips trailed down my neck.

My hips moved more rapidly, searching.

"Need more?" Vaughn asked huskily.

I nodded, not able to disguise my pants.

"She needs you," Luc said, his fingers coming back to circle that bundle of nerves.

Vaughn moved in a flash, shucking his pants and tugging me towards the end of the bed. His tip teased my entrance. My legs hooked around his waist, spurring him on.

He thrust inside me in a slow glide. One that stretched and filled me in the best way imaginable. My eyes couldn't help but flutter closed.

Vaughn picked up a rhythm that had a storm gathering inside me, a tornado of sensations engulfing me. But it wasn't just Vaughn creating it. It was all of them. Each one spurring the storm on in their own unique way that spoke to my body and soul.

They were everywhere, my mates, around me, inside me, consuming me. Sparks danced off my skin, surrounding us all. They swirled, creating a cascade of light. But more than that, they created a wave of sensation enveloping us. And as I spiraled and frayed, I took them all with me.

CHAPTER THIRTY-SIX

I SLID THE SCRAMBLE FROM THE SKILLET ONTO A PLATTER just as the timer dinged. Grabbing the pot holders, I opened the oven and pulled out the biscuits.

Footsteps sounded on the stairs.

"I smell something amazing," Anson said.

"Hopefully it tastes decent."

Luc moved in behind me, wrapping his arms around my waist and resting his chin on my shoulder. "It looks great. I thought you said you didn't really know how to cook."

I placed the biscuits one by one in a towel-lined bowl. "I don't know the fancy stuff, but I've got the basics covered. I had to learn when my mom stopped functioning."

My heart squeezed at using the word. My father had done what Mason had instructed and stayed away. I hadn't heard a word from him or my mom. I didn't even know if she was still in the hospital. In spite of all the awful things that had happened, I still wanted them to be okay.

There was anger and hurt in the mix too, but they were my last real tie to Lacey. It was impossible for me to wish any true ill will towards them. There would likely never be a time where I didn't miss the family we used to be.

Luc brushed the hair away from my face. "It's okay to miss them."

Anson's brows pulled together. "Your adoptive parents?"

I nodded. "I know they both did horrible things, but that wasn't how they were growing up. They were amazing. I think losing Lace just…broke them."

I never wanted to get to that place. The one where I became a person I didn't recognize out of grief. I wanted to hold onto who I was, to be the person Lacey loved.

Luc pressed a kiss to the side of my face, holding me more tightly. "You can't turn off loving someone, not if that emotion is true. You loved them your whole life, that doesn't disappear. I don't think you'd want it to."

He had a point there. I turned, burrowing into his embrace. Anson moved in behind me, closing the circle. I was completely cocooned in their arms.

There was a peace that had settled over me since last night. All of us coming together in a physical manifestation of the love we shared. There was a rightness that I was so completely secure in.

"Love you guys," I mumbled against Luc's chest.

"We love you too. And we're here no matter what. If you want to talk about them or Lacey, we'll always listen," Luc said.

Anson kissed the top of my head. "You're never alone, even in the confusing muck of family."

He understood that better than most.

I turned, lifting my gaze to Anson's. "Have you heard from your mom at all?"

He shook his head. "Not since that postcard from Switzerland."

I wanted to give the woman a swift kick. She hadn't batted an eye when he'd moved out of their home to live with people she didn't even know.

I linked my fingers with his, squeezing. "We're building something beautiful here. And strong. It won't collapse under the strain of whatever's ahead."

Emotion blazed in Anson's eyes. "You're right. It feels stronger than ever."

My mouth curved into a smile. "It does, doesn't it?"

I climbed out of Anson's SUV and was engulfed in a Cass hug. "I'm so sorry about yesterday."

"I'm fine, promise." My body had healed completely overnight. I didn't even have any bruises around my neck. But I still fought a shudder as Chris' face flashed in my mind. The fact that I'd have to see him on the daily until we graduated was not something I was looking forward to.

"I'd like to rearrange Sadie's face and give Chris a castration with no anesthesia."

Ridge's lips twitched as he wrapped an arm around his mate. "She's bloodthirsty when it comes to the people she cares about."

I chuckled. "I'm glad she's on my team."

Jack grinned. "You should be." The smile slipped from his face. "I'm glad you're okay."

"Me too."

"I'm just glad that Anson didn't murder anyone," Ridge said.

Anson slung an arm over my shoulders. "It was touch and go there for a moment."

Looks passed between the guys, and I knew that if Chris started anything today, he wouldn't make it until last period.

"Please try not to get arrested," I said with a sigh.

Keene shot me a grin. "Have a little faith in us, Ro. We'd never get caught."

"Boys," I grumbled and Cass laughed.

"They do keep things interesting."

I glared at her. "Don't encourage them."

She held up both hands. "Sorry. It's good that they're protective though."

"Protective or obsessive? I almost had to sedate Vaughn to keep him from coming to school with us."

Cass let out a strangled sound. "That would've been a bloodbath, for sure."

I pinched the bridge of my nose, and Anson chuckled in my ear. I could only imagine what chaos that would've brought.

The warning bell sounded.

Holden inclined his head towards the school. "We better get going."

Our group headed in the direction of the front doors. I didn't miss how all of them surrounded me. I let out a low growl. "Chris and his crazy pants girlfriend aren't going to attack me in the middle of school."

A muscle in Luc's jaw fluttered. "We aren't taking any chances."

It was going to be a long day.

Ridge opened the door and held it for all of us. We stepped inside, the halls bustling with students hurrying to their classes.

We made our way towards astronomy, but my steps faltered as I caught sight of Chris standing with his friends.

His eyes went wide as he saw us coming down the hallway, and then he began to tremble. I started to feel bad for him, but then remembered the vile words he'd whispered in my ear. My stomach pitched and I found my mad.

Anson glared at him and Chris' shaking intensified. A wet spot formed on his jeans, only growing as we got closer.

Cass let out a loud laugh. "Did he just piss himself?"

"Serves him right," Anson gritted out.

The guys surrounding Chris began to laugh and point, other students joining in. He took off down the hallway, his head ducked low, one hand covering his crotch as people cackled and shouted taunts. That was what happened when you were an asshole to everyone. They'd turn on you the moment you showed weakness.

I turned my gaze away from the pitiful sight. Something told me we wouldn't have to worry about Chris again. Now it was just Sadie. There was no telling how she'd react to the events of yesterday. They could've scared her straight. Or she could double down on her reign of terror.

Movement caught in the corner of my vision. Sadie's bitch squad, with the queen herself at the helm. Her eyes jumped around the hall, locking on us. She paled.

One of Chris' friends knocked the hat she was wearing off her head as he passed. My jaw dropped. Cass sucked in an audible breath.

Sadie's usually sleek blonde hair looked as if she'd stuck her finger in a light socket. I guessed she had been electrocuted by my gift.

Students around her started to giggle and whisper. She scrambled to pick up the hat and pull it back over her head.

"Nice hair, Sadie," one of the boys hollered.

She scowled at him and hurried into the classroom.

Cass turned slowly in my direction. "Tell me that was you."

I grimaced. "I think so."

"Girl, do not feel bad. She tried to have you attacked and kicked out of school. A bad hair day is the least she deserves."

Cass was right, and I couldn't think of a more fitting punishment for someone as vain as Sadie. The scales were evening out. I just had to hope they'd reach Kaleb too.

CHAPTER THIRTY-SEVEN

MY FOOTSTEPS SLOWED AS I APPROACHED KEENE'S bedroom. We'd all slept together in my room each night, but we'd sometimes find our separate corners during the evening if there were school projects or studying that required a lot of focus.

I stepped into the doorway, leaning against the frame. Keene's fingers flew across his keyboard, his ice-blue eyes riveted on the screen of his computer. A lock of his dark hair swept across his forehead.

My stomach tightened as I took in his beauty. No guy wanted to be known as beautiful but that was what Keene was. So handsome, it nearly stole my breath.

His nose twitched and I knew he must've caught my scent. "Come in, Ro."

"I don't want to interrupt."

He inclined his head towards another chair in the corner without taking his eyes off the screen. "You won't be. Pull up a chair."

I lifted the seat and set it down next to Keene's. "What are you working on?"

The vast collection of internet windows didn't look like anything for school.

"I'm hunting."

My hands tightened on the arms of the chair as I sat. "Kaleb?"

Keene nodded. "He knows how to live off the grid, but there's always a trail."

"Will you talk me through it?"

We hadn't had a lot of time or opportunity to get to know the daily minutia of each other's lives after we bonded. We'd been so wrapped up in one drama after another that there hadn't been time to learn about our hobbies and interests. But I wanted to know everything about my bond.

"Sure." He clicked over to a map on the screen. "Remember what Abigail said about that place Kaleb used to go to growing up?"

"Somewhere in Idaho."

"She said it was on a lake and near a mountain." He zoomed out on the map. "I'm logging all of the possibilities."

I stared at the image on the screen. "There have to be a lot of options."

"There are, but I'm also in Kaleb's bank accounts."

My eyes widened. "You can do that?"

Keene sent me a devilish grin. "I can do lots of things."

Heat pooled in my belly, but I forced myself to focus on the task at hand. "If you're in his bank account, can't you just see where in Idaho he's used his card?"

"I can and there are a bunch of hits, but none of those places fit what we're looking for."

"Damn." For a second, I'd felt a glimmer of hope.

"I have an idea."

"Tell me."

Keene lifted a piece of paper and set it between us. The printout of the map had a series of red Xs all over it. "These are where he's used a card."

There were a few that appeared to be near lakes, but none of those had a mountain nearby.

"I think Kaleb is smart enough to know someone might break into his accounts to look for a trail. If this really is his hidey hole, he's probably not using anything traceable in the vicinity. He probably switches to cash and burner phones. Likely has his enforcers do the same."

I looked up at Keene. "Then why are you still mapping the places he used his card?"

"I'm hoping it will give us a pattern. Want to help?"

"Sure."

Keene smiled. "I always wanted a sidekick."

"Hey, I think I'm superhero material in my own right."

He leaned in and took my mouth in a kiss. That steady pressure that made my toes curl threatened to swallow me whole. When Keene finally pulled away, I was breathless.

"A distracting as hell superhero."

I chuckled. "Right back at you." I picked up the red pen Keene had been using. "Ready when you are."

He brought up a browser that seemed to be a bank interface. "All right. Did I mark off Idaho Falls?"

I scanned the printout. "Yup."

"Coeur d'Alene?"

I ran my finger over the paper, scanning the cities and towns. "Found it. That one isn't marked."

"Put a red X through it." Keene typed on his keyboard. "Nampa."

"Found it and marked it."

We continued like that for another hour at least. Based on the number of hits, we had to have covered years of Kaleb's transactions. Keene hit the return key and sighed. "Okay, I think that's it."

I leaned back in my chair, stretching. "Now what? It just looks like a jumble of red marks to me."

"Now we look for the patterns."

Keene leaned over the map and picked up a pencil. As he studied the printout, he began drawing circles. With each swipe of his pencil he connected another series of red Xs. Before long, the paper began to resemble a Venn diagram.

I leaned closer, trying to get a look at the center.

"When you think about it from a logical perspective, there has to be a buffer around where he's hiding." Keene's pencil kept drawing the circles tighter and tighter.

With each pass of lead against paper, an empty space began to appear. I sucked in a breath. "That's a lake."

"A small one, but I'd say it qualifies." He dropped the pencil and turned back to the computer screen, pulling up the map. "What's the name?"

I squinted at the tiny letters. "Green Lake."

"Not very original," Keene muttered as he typed.

"We aren't looking for original. We're looking for something that could house a criminal mastermind."

He chuckled and then stilled. "Holy crap."

"What?"

Keene typed furiously for a few moments and then scanned the screen. "Green Lake was purchased by a corporation for private development fifteen years ago. It's no longer open to the public and locked gates prevent any road access." He looked up, meeting my gaze. "It's at the base of a series of mountains."

"What's the name of the corporation?"

Keene turned back to the screen, searching. The muscles across his shoulders pulled tight. "Kal-tech."

Nausea swept through me. "Of course he wouldn't be able to resist naming even a shell company after himself."

"What an asshole."

"The biggest."

Keene shifted so that he was facing me. He tugged my chair closer to himself. "We found him."

A shudder shot through me. "He's there. I don't know how to explain it, but I just know."

Keene's hands came up to frame my face. "We're going to stop him, Ro. Then you and everyone else will be free."

"Thanks to you. We would still be fumbling around in the dark if you hadn't thought of this idea."

The corner of his mouth kicked up. "I am a computer genius."

I leaned forward, skating my lips across his. "You are."

He grinned against my mouth. "Is this my reward?"

"No. But this is." I sunk to the carpet. My fingers going to the button on Keene's jeans.

His hand closed around mine. "Rowan, I was joking."

My eyes lifted to his. "I'm not."

Keene's length strained against his boxers. I pulled it out and closed my lips around his tip. Keene let out a groan that had me squeezing my thighs together.

I took note of every shudder and hissed out breath as my tongue swirled. I tested suction and flicks of my tongue. That invisible cord in me wound tighter as Keene's sounds of pleasure floated through the air.

"Rowan."

My name was a plea on his lips.

I released my grip on his shaft. "Yes?"

His eyes hooded and in the next moment, I was airborne. Then Keene's hands were on my workout shorts, pulling them down. His fingers dove between my legs and his eyes flared. "So wet. Did that turn you on?"

I bit my lip. "I like knowing I can bring you pleasure."

Keene's gaze went arctic as he trailed that wetness to my clit, circling. "I've never known pleasure like what you bring me."

I couldn't help the shiver that rocked through me. But it wasn't enough. I wanted what I always did. To feel one of my mates moving inside me. "Keene, please."

"More?"

"You."

That was all it took. In a flash, Keene was pushing inside me. My legs circled his waist as he pumped into me, desperate and searching.

Keene's fingers dug into my hips. "Fuck, Ro. You feel like heaven."

His words had me arching into him, meeting Keene thrust for thrust. There was such hunger in each move. A need to cement ourselves inside one another, so deep we'd never escape, because we didn't want to.

Keene's thumb circled my clit. "Reach for it, Ro. Come with me."

It was all I needed, the words, the sensation, and Keene. I spiraled, flickers of light cascading over my vision. "Keene."

He let out a curse, thrusting into me once more, then collapsing to the bed. He rolled so that I was on top of him and we both struggled to catch our breath.

Keene's hand stroked up and down my back. "That was—"

"Amazing."

He chuckled, sending more delicious aftershocks through me. "It was that."

"Love this life with you."

Keene's fingers stilled. "I can't imagine anything better."

I pressed a kiss to the underside of his jaw.

Keene groaned as he slid from my body, and I winced at the loss of him. Somehow, I already wanted him again. He tugged me into his bathroom. Wetting a rag, he pressed it between my thighs. "Tender?"

"Just sensitive."

Keene's gentle care made my heart ache.

He handed me a pair of his sweats. "Here. These should work for now. I think I ripped your shorts."

I chuckled as we both pulled on sweats. "Worth it."

He kissed the side of my head. "Damn straight."

I felt the telltale knocking in my mind of an incoming message. I opened the pack link and Mason's voice filled my head. *Ivan is here.*

The rest of the Quad? Holden asked.

He came alone. He said he wants to talk to Rowan.

CHAPTER THIRTY-EIGHT

THE GUYS SURROUNDED ME AS WE SPILLED OUT OF THE SUV. The lights from the lodge glowed in the dark, warm and reassuring. But the truth was we had no idea what we were about to face.

Vaughn scowled at the building. "This is a bad idea. It's probably a trap."

I slid my hand into his. "Ivan's here alone. I have all of you and the enforcers. We'll be fine."

He tugged me closer to him. "I don't like it."

"Of course you don't. You don't like anyone but our bond."

His lips twitched. "I'm still iffy on anyone but you."

"Hey." Anson's mouth pulled into an exaggerated pout. "I thought we were on our way to becoming besties."

"Let's focus," Holden said as we made our way up the steps. "We need to be on the lookout for any signs that Ivan is working with Kaleb. It's vital that we figure out who is on his side."

My stomach cramped at the thought of someone supporting the kidnapping of women and slaughtering of innocent shifters. All of us went quiet as Luc opened the front door.

The warm glow of the lights inside illuminated a tense circle. Mason, Mac, and a handful of enforcers surrounded Ivan. He seemed remarkably calm for the scenario.

"Thank you for coming, Rowan."

Ivan didn't turn around before speaking the words. Whether he could scent me or simply sensed me with a gift I couldn't understand, I didn't know.

"Why are you here?" I didn't have time or energy to play games with members of the Quad. And I was through with them attempting to use me.

Ivan turned around slowly. He wore a simple linen outfit. Loose pants and tunic top. Something that made him look like he was about to embark on a meditation retreat instead of heading into enemy territory. "I'm here to speak frankly."

Keene let out a low growl, taking a step forward. "Like we would trust anything that comes out of your mouth."

Ivan held up two hands. "I understand that. Just listen and you can judge for yourselves." He took a breath, readying himself. "When Mason came to the Quad to share what had happened to Rowan, I honestly believed Kaleb was being framed."

"Bullshit," Vaughn snapped. "He dropped off the face of the planet the day we rescued Rowan. That didn't seem suspicious to you?"

"He had his explanation. That a few of his enforcers had betrayed him, and he was trying to weed out the traitors in his pack. It has happened before, that an alpha has convinced someone to turn on their own." Ivan's gaze swept around the room. "It has happened in your own pack."

My hands fisted at the memory of Sam's attack. Of Jaz's betrayal.

Ivan glanced at Mason. "You are missing two wolves, are you not?"

Mason stiffened. "That isn't a secret. We've put out a bounty on them."

"Jasmine and Coby have pledged their loyalty to Kaleb."

Holden let out a snarl. "Where are they?"

"Somewhere you won't be able to reach them without help."

"Your version of help could send us right over a cliff," Anson bit out.

Ivan shook his head. There was a weariness to him. One that spoke of a bone-deep fatigue. "Our world is sick. It has been for generations. The quest for ultimate power has left us out of balance."

He turned to me. "Has anyone told you how shifters first came to be?"

"No," I answered quietly.

Ivan's gaze went unfocused, as if he were seeing a scene play out in front of his eyes. "Generations ago, that delicate balance was at risk. Lands that had once been dominated by animals were being overrun with humans. These humans took and took from the land without giving back. When an entire pack of wolves was slaughtered, the fates were not happy. They weaved their magic, binding wolf with man, and shifters were born."

He leaned back against the sofa as if needing the support. "For a time, it helped. Man grew to understand animal and there was peace. Balance. The fates rewarded their new creation with gifts. As long as balance remained in their ranks and with the world around them, those gifts would grow."

"But now they're dying." My words slipped out.

"They are. The fates aren't happy with us. They haven't been for some time. This is their message to us, but we aren't heeding it."

"I can't imagine they were all that thrilled with the king and court system Kaleb is so obsessed with either."

Ivan's eyes flared. "You know about that?"

I let out a chuckle that was void of amusement. "Kaleb won't shut up about it."

Ivan's mouth pressed into a hard line. "There was a time when the royal system worked. It wasn't as we think of kings and queens today. They took the well-being of the packs on their shoulders, determined to protect and care for their people. They helped broker peace when there were issues and made sure that precious balance remained in place."

"What happened?"

His knuckles bleached white as he gripped the couch tighter. "The quest for power and control. The kings that followed wanted all of the benefits with none of the hard work. They didn't care for their people's well-being, only what the people could provide them."

Holden moved in closer to me. "There was an uprising, which is when the council and Quad were created."

Ivan smiled at Holden. "You've been studying."

"Our past shapes our future."

"You'll be a wonderful leader when it's your time, pup."

Holden glared at him. "I'm not a pup."

"Maybe not. But to an old fart like me, you're all pups."

Anson stifled a laugh.

"But the Quad is basically a four-pronged king," I argued. "How is that any better?"

"You have a point there," Ivan said with a sigh. "The trials were supposed to reveal those destined to lead…"

"But they only show you those who are the strongest or most gifted. That can easily be someone who is power-hungry, not who has the best interests of the shifter world at heart," I finished for him.

"You're right."

"How do we remove Kaleb from the Quad?" I had to believe there was a loophole. Some way to cut him off from any semblance of power.

Ivan's gaze zeroed in on me. "There's only one way. You have to kill him."

CHAPTER THIRTY-NINE

O PENING THE DOOR, I STEPPED OUT ON TO THE BACK porch. Early morning mist swept out from the forests. It swirled in little funnels and then wafted into the air. I pulled Holden's sweatshirt tighter around me. We'd opted to stay in his old room at the lodge last night, wanting to be close in case anything happened.

"Are you an early riser too, Rowan?"

Ivan's voice startled me into sloshing a little of my hot chocolate over the edge of my mug. "One of these days, I'm going to get those shifter senses in working order."

He chuckled and patted the Adirondack chair next to him. "Join me."

I didn't see the harm in it. I could just glimpse a couple of enforcers through the trees, so I lowered myself into the seat.

Ivan tilted his head towards the woods. "My permanent company."

"Do you blame them? We don't know your true motivation for being here."

"Fair point." He leaned back against the chair and lifted his mug to his lips, drinking deep. "Tea always soothes the worst of the world's problems. Don't you think?"

I lifted my own mug. "I'm going for hot chocolate this morning."

"Always a winner. I'm partial to chocolate."

"Then you're not stupid."

Ivan let out a chortle. "I'm glad to pass muster."

"That remains to be seen."

None of us had revealed to Ivan that we had likely found Kaleb's hideout or discussed any plans for how we might smoke him out of the hidey hole. As much as I wanted to believe Ivan might want to help, I wasn't sure.

"I thought it was Gregor pushing the royal agenda behind the scenes."

I turned at Ivan's words, taking in the lined planes of his face. "He does seem like someone who would want the world to worship at his feet."

"You've got him pegged."

My mouth puckered as if I'd tasted something sour, the memories of Gregor's visits here swimming through my mind. "He certainly deserves a permanent case of diarrhea."

Ivan choked on a laugh. "I like you, Rowan."

"I want to like you too. But I'm still not sure if I can trust you."

"That's smart. You shouldn't trust anyone but your bond right now. They are who's safe."

"That's no way to live." I didn't want to walk through life constantly questioning people's intentions.

"No, it's not."

Grief swept through Ivan so strong and fast, I could feel it as if it were a physical wave. "Someone betrayed you?"

His mouth curved into a sad smile. "Living as long as I have, lots of people have betrayed me."

I stayed quiet, hoping it would coax more out of Ivan.

"My mother was an energy bender."

I sucked in an audible breath. My brain began to whirl at a rapid rate, a million questions swirling. Ivan had to have so many of the answers I sought.

He shook his head slowly. "She was taken when I was just seven."

My chest constricted. "Because of her gift?"

"Yes. I never saw her again. She was used and abused, forced to bend to a powerful alpha's will. By the time my fathers figured out where she was, it was too late."

"I'm so sorry." I wanted to reach out to Ivan, to pull the old man into a hug. But I held back.

"I swore then and there that I would never have children of my own. Wouldn't risk that they too would have that gift. One that was so deeply hungered for."

I swallowed hard. "It's likely you have the same or similar gift as your parents."

I'd known there was a chance. Mason had said as much when they first explained the gifts to me. But we hadn't known what I was then.

Nausea swept through me as I imagined putting my child at risk for simply existing. Yet I couldn't imagine not having a family with the guys I loved so much. Not anytime soon, but someday. My heart ached at the idea of not fulfilling that dream.

"That was my choice, Rowan. It doesn't have to be yours.

My hope is that we can change our world, right this wrong path that we're on."

"We can't control the choices of individuals, that hunger for more. It's wired into some people."

Ivan shifted in his chair, turning towards me. "That may be the case, but we can lift up those who have been powerless."

My thumb stroked the side of my mug as I considered his words. "Those without gifts."

"And those who are part of small packs."

"Like the Canadian pack."

Ivan stiffened, his jaw going hard. "Exactly like them."

"And how do you propose doing that?"

"First thing is that there must be swift punishment for anyone who would perpetrate such actions. It shouldn't matter if they are rogues or part of a pack, there must be a severe price to pay."

I didn't disagree with Ivan, but the idea of solving our problems with more violence didn't seem right either.

Ivan reached out and patted my hand. "Sometimes force is all some individuals will understand."

I knew that was true when it came to Kaleb. He wouldn't be stopped by a convincing argument. "We have to be a united front. That means the majority of the packs being on the same page. It doesn't seem like there's great communication between them. The Quad talks to the council but doesn't always explain their judgments. And not every pack has a representative on the council."

"Have you ever considered going into politics?"

I snorted. "No, thank you."

"You should reconsider. Those are great points. There has to be a way to get the Quad's message straight to all shifters. Video casts perhaps."

"And there needs to be a way for every shifter to share their opinion or ask questions if they want to."

Ivan's lips pursed. "I'm not sure how Gregor and Cinna will feel about that."

"Then you'll have to convince them. It's time for real change, and for that to happen, everyone has to have a voice."

"I don't disagree, but we have another pressing issue to deal with first."

My stomach cramped. "Kaleb."

"You are the only one who can stop him."

"I know." I simply had to be brave enough to do it.

"Your bond must fuel you. It is only through them that you will be strong enough to take him down. Especially if he has ventured into black magic like I suspect."

"He has."

Ivan straightened, his eyes narrowing on me. "What do you know?"

I toyed with the handle of my mug. "He has reached me in dreams. Physically hurt me."

Ivan's eyes went wide. "What do you mean?"

I set my mug down and lifted my T-shirt and sweatshirt. "He can injure me in my dreams."

Ivan scowled at the mark. He reached out a hand and then paused. "May I?"

I bit my lip and then nodded.

He closed his eyes and held his hand just shy of my skin, where the lightning bolt was etched. Heat hummed around the mark and my flesh began to vibrate. My jaw dropped open, a gasp slipping free. The mark was disappearing. After a few moments, it was gone altogether.

"How?"

Ivan smiled at me. "I have a healing gift. One that can mend injuries from magic." His smile melted into a frown. "That was dark magic. It would allow him to track you wherever you went."

"Abigail told me as much. But I didn't know there was a way to get it off."

"He won't be able to sense you now, but he'll also know I aided you. It might be a push in the right direction. It may force him to tip his hand or to reveal who else is working with him."

"I hate that I have his blood in me."

Ivan reached out, taking my hand in his. "Rowan. You aren't just made of him. You are also made of a mother who gave up everything to protect you. And most importantly, you are your own creation. A culmination of trials and tribulations. Choices and experiences. I have faith that you will find the path you need."

I gripped his hand harder. "I'm scared that I'll take the wrong one or won't be strong enough in the moment."

"That doubt tells me you are exactly who we need to fight this battle."

CHAPTER FORTY

I slipped into Holden's room as the guys were getting ready. Luc moved to me instantly, pulling me into his arms. "What is it?"

"Nothing bad. I just had an emotional conversation with Ivan."

"Why were you talking to him? Especially alone," Vaughn gritted out.

"I wasn't alone. There were enforcers in the woods."

Holden pulled a shirt over his head. "What did he have to say?"

I leaned into Luc's hold. "Did you know his mother was an energy bender?"

"No shit?" Anson asked.

"She was taken when he was little. She never made it home."

"Ro…" Luc held me tighter against him.

Keene scowled. "He shouldn't be filling your head with that shit."

"It wasn't like that, I swear. It was a good conversation, it just wasn't a light one."

None of the guys looked convinced.

I sighed. "I want to go see Abigail again."

Ivan's words played in my head about half of my makeup coming from her. And that wasn't a half I'd explored nearly enough. Maybe because each visit ended in disaster, maybe because I was afraid to hope. That had proved to be a dangerous emotion in my world. Every parent I'd had in my life had abandoned me in one way or another. It was terrifying to let myself ask her to stay.

"I don't know if that's such a good idea," Vaughn said.

"No," Luc argued. "We should go."

I pressed a kiss to the underside of his jaw. "Thanks."

"Then we all go," Keene said.

Anson grabbed a sweatshirt and threw it over his shoulder. "That's fine with me. But we're getting burgers on the way back."

I grinned. "Always thinking with your stomach."

"No, sometimes I'm thinking with my—"

"Anson!" I smacked his chest and the rest of the guys burst out laughing. It was exactly what we needed.

I stared out at the back patio where Abigail was painting. The air was chilly, but with the sun shining and our shifter heat, she wouldn't feel it.

Luc kissed the top of my head. "Go. We'll be right here if you need us."

"Keene and I will patrol the perimeter in wolf form," Vaughn said.

I nodded, not taking my eyes off the woman who was my mother. I pressed down on the door handle and stepped outside.

I made no effort to be quiet as I walked across the stone patio. Startling Abigail was the last thing I wanted to do.

Her grip on the paintbrush tightened as she turned around. "Rowan."

"Hi." I still wasn't sure what moniker to use. None of them felt exactly right.

Abigail's gaze lifted to the doors behind me. "Your mates can come out if they'd like."

"They wanted to give us some time alone."

"But not entirely alone."

My hands fisted at my sides. "Do you blame them?"

Her lips thinned into a hard line. "I guess not." She turned towards a smattering of patio furniture. "Would you like to sit?"

"Sure."

Abigail moved in that direction, and I couldn't help but notice that she seemed more with it today. More lucid, maybe? But I also remembered from my first visit that lucidity could turn on a dime.

I wrapped the ends of my bracelets around my finger. "What have you been painting?"

"Landscapes mostly. Things from memory during my therapy sessions."

A pang lit along my sternum. I could only imagine the kind of memories she was giving voice to at those times. How scared she must've been.

"I draw."

As soon as the words were out, I felt incredibly lame for sharing them. But Abigail's eyes brightened. "Really? Pencil or...?"

"Oil pastels. I like how they layer."

Her mouth curved into a smile. "I always liked how tactile that medium was."

Hope bubbled up inside me at this point of connection. "Me too. No mistake is permanent."

"You can always just smudge it into something else."

"Exactly."

She sighed. "I wish life were that way."

"In some ways, it is. We learn and grow from our mistakes."

Abigail shook her head. "But some are too big." She lifted her eyes to mine and they shone in the late morning light. "I don't know if I made the worst kind of mistake with you. Maybe I shouldn't have run. Maybe I should've gone to Mason as soon as I knew I was pregnant. But I was so ashamed of the choices I'd made."

I reached out, taking her hand in mine. "You did what you thought was best. You gave everything to protect me. I couldn't ask for more."

That didn't mean I didn't have what-ifs. I longed for memories I'd never have. Growing up in the pack, alongside my mates. But I also couldn't wish my childhood away because it would mean erasing Lacey. All I could do was be grateful for the here and now.

Abigail's hand shook as she squeezed mine. "That's what I was trying to do. It killed me to give you up. I don't think I was ever the same after that."

My heart broke for her. I couldn't imagine what that must've been like. What sort of deep pain made itself at home in your soul when you lost a child.

"Maybe we could start over?"

Abigail's brows pulled together. "What do you mean?"

"We can't get those years back, but we can get to know each other now. It won't erase what happened, but it could give us something beautiful now."

Her eyes filled. "I'd love that, Rowan."

The first steps were tenuous. Questions that were careful not to step on toes. But after a while, we found our rhythm. I shared funny stories about Lacey. We traded lists of favorites. She told me about all of the places she lived while she was on the run. And for the first time, I got to know my mother.

I was so lost in our storytelling, I didn't hear Holden approach until he was steps away. I lifted my gaze to him and the smile fled my face as I took in his serious expression. "What's wrong?"

"We have to go back to pack territory. The rest of the Quad is here."

CHAPTER FORTY-ONE

ANSON TOOK THE TURNS BACK TOWARDS PACK territory much more quickly than the drive to the hospital. I wasn't sure if it was the knowledge of the Quad members waiting for us or the quick movements of the SUV that had me more nauseated. My hand slipped into Holden's. "Did your dad say anything else?"

He shook his head. "Just to hurry back."

"But no Kaleb?" My nausea intensified simply saying his name. The idea that he might just show up and pretend he'd done nothing wrong swirled in my mind.

"No," Holden gritted out. "He's staying hidden like the coward he is."

Coward was exactly the word for Kaleb. He was the personification of it.

Luc took my other hand, clasping it between his own. "How was the time with your mom?"

I blinked a few times, trying to clear the spiral my mind was on. "It was good. She seemed better today...clearer. It'll take time, but for the first time I felt..."

"Hope?" he finished for me.

Warmth bloomed in my chest. "Hope."

Just naming the emotion had fear battling at the edges of my consciousness. I wanted so badly to have a parent in my life that I could be close to, but I'd been wounded so many times before. Burned in a way that had me cautious of putting my hand too close to the flame.

"It's okay to want her in your life. To believe that relationship can be more," he said softly.

I leaned into Luc. There were people who would've been freaked out by Luc's gift or the fact that, more and more, the guys were able to sense what I was thinking and feeling, but to me, it was nothing but comfort.

Vaughn leaned forward from the seat behind us and brushed the hair away from my neck. He pressed his lips to the skin there, lingering. "She did seem better today. I can sense volatility in other shifters, and it was much lower in her."

My chest ached but in a beautifully painful way. I never took Vaughn's touches for granted. I'd lived without them for so long. Every time he sought me out for the most casual of caresses, it was the greatest gift. But his touch paired with words of reassurance? It was almost more than I could take.

I tipped my head back and reached my lips up to his. "Love you."

He grinned against my mouth. "Love you too."

"You know, I'm going to quit driving if the fun is always in the back seat," Anson griped.

Keene chuckled. "I knew I should've gone in the third row with Vaughn."

"Sure, leave me to be chauffeur."

I leaned forward and pressed a kiss to Anson's shoulder. "I'll reward you later. Promise."

His mouth curved. "I like the sound of that."

The traces of humor fled the vehicle as Anson slowed to a stop at the gate. He punched in a code and it swung open.

My stomach pitched again. "Tell me it's going to be fine."

No one said a word for a moment. Luc squeezed my hand. "Whatever it is, we'll figure it out together."

I was done doing anything lone-wolf style. I'd learned the hard way what a mistake that was. The bond was my strength. It was all of ours. Not just in the supercharging of our gifts, but in the way we all balanced each other out. We were healthier and happier when we were one.

Anson pulled the SUV to a stop in front of the lodge, and I swallowed hard as we all climbed out. My muscles had a rigidness to them as I forced myself to head towards the steps.

The guys surrounded me as they always did. Vaughn took point, leading our group. He opened the door, stepping inside. The tension in the room wafted over me. Luc winced next to me, and I instantly took his hand, healing the worst of his pain. He sent me a grateful smile.

No one sat. That was the first thing I noticed. They'd been waiting for at least thirty minutes, but no one had relaxed enough to take a seat.

I glanced at Ivan, trying to get a read on him. I hated to think that he might've brought Gregor and Cinna here. That he might've only been the first wave of a probe into our midst. But he looked pissed as hell that the other two were here.

"Rowan," Gregor said in greeting, four guards surrounding him.

I gave him a nod but didn't bother saying his name.

A muscle in his cheek ticked. "You seem to have made a full recovery from your…*ordeal*."

He said the last word as if he doubted I'd ever been taken. My hands curled into fists as both Vaughn and Anson let out low growls.

Cinna studied me carefully. For the first time since meeting her, she didn't seem flighty and easily distractable. She was on alert. "Do you wish to change your story?"

"And what *story* is that?"

She straightened, her own guard moving in closer. "That one of our Quad ranks would stoop to attempting to kidnap you."

"Kaleb did kidnap me. He assigned guards to torture me."

Gregor scoffed. "He has been in our leadership ranks for years." He glared at Mason. "But *someone* is intent on discrediting him. Attempting to take his power. We won't let that happen."

Ivan pushed off the couch he leaned against. "We may have missed the signs where Kaleb is concerned."

Cinna's jaw fell open. "You can't honestly believe that."

Gregor stepped towards Ivan, his teeth bared. "You would side with those who try to undo us?"

"I side with the truth. As we have vowed to do. I side with the good of our people who are being neglected."

Cinna's mouth opened and closed as she struggled for words. "Of course that's our vow. It's what we're doing. We must protect the shifter community from those who would overthrow it—"

"And that's Kaleb." Mason's voice boomed across the room. "Kaleb wants absolute power. A return to the monarchy. He wants to be king."

"That's absurd," Cinna said.

But there was a flicker of something in Gregor's eyes that told me this wasn't news to him. The only thing I couldn't figure out was what would be in it for Gregor. He wouldn't want to bow to Kaleb.

Gregor squared his shoulders, facing Mason. "You push too far. You have broken the sacred rules of our world."

"By speaking the truth?"

"By spreading your foul lies," Gregor growled. "Mason Pierce, you are under arrest for high treason."

CHAPTER FORTY-TWO

THE ENTIRE ROOM FROZE AND THEN BURST INTO action. Mac slid in front of Mason, shielding him as other enforcers poured into the space. Energy crackled from my fingertips as the Quad's guard braced for battle.

"Stop!" Ivan boomed.

His powerful voice drew everyone up short. He strode through the crowd, placing himself between Mason and Gregor. "On what grounds?"

"Is betrayal of the Quad not reason enough?" Gregor barked.

"Bringing concerns before the Quad, the reporting of a crime—these are not betrayals. These actions show that Mason places the ultimate trust in our leadership. He is trusting *us* to make things right."

"You believe that Kaleb could be behind this?" Cinna spluttered.

Ivan held up both hands as if the action could soothe her. "I believe that we need to look into all the possibilities. I also believe that there is no malice in Mason's actions. If Kaleb isn't responsible, then he has been tricked into believing he was."

I could've kissed Ivan in that moment. I knew he was in a precarious spot, but he'd managed to weave through his loyalties while remaining true to his character.

Gregor's hands fisted at his sides. "Have you been taken in by the Ridgewood pack? Lulled into stupidity? Or do you work against us, as they do?"

Rage blazed from Ivan's eyes. It was the ultimate insult. "I would never throw over the well-being of my people in the pursuit of power. The same isn't true for others in this room."

"If you have an accusation, state it plainly."

"I'm still gathering my evidence."

Ivan's words were a threat. A vow that he would find the truth.

Energy crackled beneath my hands.

Hold it steady, Luc spoke in my mind.

I opened a link to my bond. *What do we do if they try to take Mason?*

My gaze flicked to Holden. His muscles were strung tight, ready to pounce if needed.

They will slaughter us if we act against them, Vaughn said. *It might not be now, but they will hunt down every last one of us as traitors and punish us to death.*

My stomach gave a vicious cramp. *Is that what they'll do to Mason?*

No. Not right away. There would be a public trial, Keene explained.

Who makes the ruling? I asked.

There was silence for a few moments and then Holden answered. *The Quad.*

This whole system was more messed up than I ever could've

imagined. A twisted façade of justice and protection. But only some members of the façade realized how fake it was. Cinna seemed oblivious to how unfair it was. Even Ivan had been blinded to much of it.

But Gregor and Kaleb? They knew and they played every part of it to their advantage. They took and took, but it would never be enough. They would always want more. It wouldn't end until there was nothing left to take, and our world was broken around us.

Ivan's voice cut through my thoughts. "If you would like to make a formal charge, please do so."

Gregor's expression faltered for a moment, but he quickly masked it. "I don't wish for us to be at odds, Ivan. I only wish to protect the Quad and our people."

He almost sounded believable, but there was a slimy edge to his words that gave him away.

Cinna sent Ivan an imploring look. "Stand with us, not against us."

He met her gaze, unwavering. "I told you, I stand with truth, with our people."

"Then it is with us that you stand," Cinna argued.

"I cannot watch as you do this to an innocent man."

Gregor grinned, but there was an ugly bent to it. "But you are outvoted. The Quad is only three when a crime has been perpetrated against the fourth member—"

"No crime has been perpetrated against Kaleb," I broke in. "He is the monster here. And so are you for pushing his agenda."

Cinna sucked in an audible breath and my bond moved in closer around me.

"Don't," Holden warned.

Gregor's eyes narrowed on me. "You don't know enough of our world yet, pup. So I will let that one slide. But you will watch your tongue."

Sparks lifted from my fingertips. Energy pulsed beneath my skin, dying to break free. It was all I could do to hold it back.

Luc took hold of my arm, pulling the worst of my rage. But it did nothing for the energy trying to get out, to get at those who were intent on doing wrong. It was as if that power had a mind of its own. An agenda of its own. It could sense the evil in Gregor and it wanted to obliterate it.

Cinna and Gregor took a step back at the sparks of light off my skin. Their guards surrounded them.

"Control your gift," Gregor barked.

I met his gaze and didn't look away. "Why?"

"If you lash out against us, the only thing that will greet you is death. And what a waste that would be."

The rage that blossomed somewhere deep inside only fueled that pool of energy. Instead of living in my center, it spread out into all my limbs.

"Shit," Anson muttered.

I glanced down to see sparks swirling all around me. They swarmed me like little lightning bugs. Dozens of them broke off, surrounding my bond as well. I had no idea what it meant, but I knew that one wrong move could make that power detonate.

Breathe. Vaughn's voice swirled about in my head. *Breathe with me. In and out. Focus on me.*

I could feel him there. Inside me. Inside my mind and inside my soul. I latched on to him. He knew better than most the dangers of losing control. I let his presence calm me and slowly the sparks faded into my skin.

Thank you, I told him as I let out a breath.

Gregor brushed invisible lint off his shirt sleeve. "The decision has been made. Mason, you will come with us by choice or by force."

"No—" Mac began, but Mason clamped a hand on his shoulder, silencing him.

"I come by choice, choosing to believe that the Quad will see the truth in this trial." He turned in our direction. "I leave willingly and I bestow Alpha status on my son, Holden."

Mason strode towards us. He gripped the back of Holden's neck and brought their foreheads together. A surge of energy filled the room. "I believe in you. Lead strong. Lead true."

Holden's eyes glistened as he met his father's gaze. "I'll make you proud."

CHAPTER FORTY-THREE

I EYED THE TABLE OF SHIFTERS THROUGH THE OPEN kitchen doors. Heads bowed over journals and pack histories, desperately searching for any precedent that would help Mason. The pack was on edge. Mason had sent out a calming message through our link before he was taken, but it could only do so much. Now that weight rested on Holden's shoulders.

My chest tightened as I took in the strain around his eyes and mouth. He never thought he'd be taking over the role of alpha so soon. Let alone in such a turbulent time.

He pointed something out in one of the books to Ivan and the table began discussing it. I forced myself to turn away, back to the task at hand. I layered deli meat on bread as Anson followed behind me with cheese. My eyes stung as I forced my tears down.

Anson stilled, dropping the slices of cheese. "Hey, what's going on?"

He turned me so that I was facing him, pulling the turkey from my hand and placing it on the cutting board. His hands slid along my neck, forcing my gaze to his. "Talk to me."

I gave my head a small shake. "It's not important."

"You being upset will always be important."

I let out a huff of air. My emotions weren't what mattered. Not when Mason was in a cell somewhere, and Kaleb was pulling strings that could end us all. "I want to help." And right now, I felt powerless.

Anson's expression gentled. "We are helping."

"Making sandwiches for people who probably don't even want them feels like a pathetic form of help."

Anson's fingers trailed along my neck in soothing strokes. "We haven't been in this world as long as the rest of them. They know the ins and outs in a way we don't. So we find a way to be useful. Making sandwiches may not seem like a lot, but it shows them we care."

I let my head fall to his chest. "You're right." I turned my head so that I could see the table but wouldn't lose contact with Anson. "I'm worried about Holden."

Anson's arms wrapped around me. "Me too. He's going to need you."

"He's going to need all of us."

"That's true, but he'll need you especially. You balance him, help tether him to the here and now. But you're also his safe place to let everything go at the end of each day. He'll need that more than ever."

It was a beautiful thing, the ebb and flow of our bond. That Anson would make sure that his bond mate had what he needed, would help me give it to him. Yet my stomach twisted with nerves. Fear that I wouldn't be enough for Holden in such a pivotal moment.

Anson squeezed me harder, seeming to read my thoughts. "You're everything he needs just as you are."

I let out a shuddering breath and then kissed the spot over Anson's heart. "Love you."

He kissed the top of my head. "Love you too."

We got back to work and made the best damn sandwiches possible. Turkey and cheese, salami, even good ole peanut butter and jelly. I poured chips into bowls, and Anson gathered sodas and waters for everyone.

We arranged a buffet of sorts on the table next to everyone, but they didn't even notice. I crossed behind Holden and slid my hands over his shoulders. "We have food for everyone. You can work while you eat or—"

Ivan shook his head. "No, a break would be good. We can go over some of what we've read and share information. We'll hit the books better with food in our bellies." He gave me a kind smile. "Thank you, Rowan."

"Anson helped too."

He turned to Anson. "Thank you too."

"I might not know all the ins and outs of shifter history and law, but I make a killer sandwich."

Luc stood and clapped Anson on the back. "I'm damn grateful for that, brother."

Holden stood, bending to kiss my temple. "Thank you, Ro."

"Are you holding up okay?"

He nodded, but nothing about his expression told me that was the truth.

"I'm here. Whatever you need, okay?"

Holden squeezed my hand and then released it. "I know."

The guys, Ivan, and Mac made their way around the buffet, ladening plates with sandwiches and chips. I followed behind, choosing a turkey sandwich for myself. I knew I needed to eat, but the idea of putting something in my stomach right now had nausea sweeping through me.

Keene placed a hand on the small of my back, ushering me to another large table where we had room to spread out with our food. "You okay?"

"Worried, but hanging in there."

His thumb swept back and forth on my back. "We'll figure it out."

I so badly wanted him to be right, but we were up against so much. I slid into the chair next to Vaughn, with Keene on my other side. Vaughn's gaze moved over my face, assessing. "Do you need to rest? This has been a long day."

I shook my head and cracked a Diet Coke. "Just need a hit of caffeine."

His mouth pulled down in a frown. "You need sleep."

"Later. Right now, I want to know what you've found."

Ivan nodded, taking a sip of his soda. "I'll rest easier when I know what's going on too. Right now, we're going over previous treason cases and studying the arguments for and against."

"We're also looking at the one time in history where a Quad member was removed from his role," Luc added.

I toyed with a potato chip. "What did he do?"

"It was still the quest for more, but that time, it was money," Luc explained. "He embezzled from the council."

"Was he tried?"

Keene nodded. "He was sentenced to life in prison."

"I thought the sentence for treason was death."

"Usually it is, but in this case, they spared him," Ivan said.

I didn't understand the rhyme or reason behind the severity

of punishments in this world. Mason was facing death simply for reporting a crime. My stomach pitched.

Vaughn's hand rubbed up and down my back as he leaned into me. "Drink a little more of your soda. It'll settle your stomach. Then you can eat."

I looked up at him. "How did you know?"

"I could feel it. Hints of nausea that I knew belonged to you."

A gentle smile curved Ivan's mouth. "It's your bond deepening. You're beginning to feel one another more. It's a wonderful gift."

The smile slipped from his face as he seemed to be listening to someone in his mind. Ivan had been communicating with his guards off and on since the other Quad members left with Mason. Each of the Quad members had some of their enforcers as guards at the prison. Ivan had told his to watch out for Mason and keep the others in line.

I gripped my can of soda tighter. "What's wrong?"

A muscle in his jaw ticked. "Mason has arrived at the prison. He's been badly beaten."

CHAPTER FORTY-FOUR

I KNOCKED SOFTLY ON HOLDEN'S DOOR. THERE WAS NO answer, but I could feel his energy inside.

I turned the knob and slowly pushed the door open. Holden sat on the end of his bed, his head in his hands. My ribs tightened around my lungs, making it hard to breathe.

Quickly, I closed the door behind me and crossed to him. I lowered myself to the bed and wrapped my arms around him. "I'm so sorry, Holden."

He didn't say a word. But after a moment, his shoulders began to shake with silent tears. I held him tighter. I didn't have anything that would make this better. I could only be here as he fell apart.

"I don't think I can do this."

I tightened my grip on him. "You can. You're already doing it."

"I'm not half the leader he is. I've always resented how much he pushed me, but for the first time, I understand why. He's hard on me because he knows our people deserve the best. He knows what it takes to give them that. I don't know if I have that in me the way he does."

I took Holden's face in my hands, forcing his gaze to mine. "You're capable of anything you set your mind to. I've seen it time and again. But you also need to give yourself grace, you're still learning—"

"I don't have time for learning. I have to lead *now*. If I make one wrong step, my father could be killed. Our entire pack could be wiped out if the Quad is feeling vindictive."

I held his face more firmly. "We aren't going to let that happen."

He leaned his forehead against mine. "You sound so sure of that."

"I am sure. I know that when we're working together, anything is possible. We just have to come up with the right path to take."

"And in the meantime, my dad is being beaten and tortured."

Memories battled at the edges of my brain. My own torture flashing in technicolor in my mind.

Holden cursed. "I'm sorry, Ro. I didn't mean to—"

"It's okay. I'm okay. It just makes me sick that Mason has been hurt. I could kill them for that. But he's with Ivan's guards now. They won't leave him alone."

"I know you're right. I just feel so damn powerless."

"We all do. There are forces at play around us that have so much control over us. But we are going to find a way to make the truth known. And we'll find a way to get to Kaleb. I wouldn't mind giving Gregor a nice shot to the balls either."

Holden chuckled. It wasn't the same full-of-life sound I was used to from him, but it was something. "I love it when you get vicious."

I nipped his bottom lip. "I'll be vicious any time you need."

Holden's mouth hovered over mine. "Need you, Ro."

"You have me."

He closed the distance, sinking into the kiss. There was a deep need in his movements, pressure and desperation. His tongue stroked mine, taking and then taking some more.

I moved so that I was straddling him. I rocked against the hard ridge in his jeans, letting out a moan at the contact.

My sounds snapped something in Holden. In a flash, I was on my back. His fingers unbuttoned my jeans and then he was pulling them and my panties down. The fabric sailed to the floor in a cascade of color.

Then Holden's head was between my legs. There was no easing into things. Holden's tongue drove into me in quick thrusts. Then he lashed out at my clit. My hands fisted in his hair.

A riot of sensations moved through me. I never knew what might come next. His fingers slid inside. Teasing, twisting, curling. I nearly bowed off the bed.

"Holden." His name was a plea for mercy on my lips.

He chuckled against my flesh, only driving me higher. He lifted his head to meet my gaze. "Did you need something?"

I scowled at him, but it was only so effective because I was panting. "You don't have to be such a show-off."

Holden grinned. "I always was an overachiever."

Having a genius in your bed didn't suck. I stifled a laugh and tugged him to me. "I want *you*."

He kissed me long and slow. "I think I can do that for you."

Holden stood. I watched in rapt fascination as he pulled his tee over his head. All that tanned skin on display. His fingers went to the button on his jeans, and I sucked in a breath as his cock sprang free. He was so damn beautiful, in every way.

His hands came to my T-shirt, lifting it up and over my head. Then my bra was free. Both of them dropped to the floor.

Holden's body covered mine. He was heat and life and love. Nothing was rushed. One hand cupped my cheek with such reverence as he slid inside. I swore I could feel his love pouring over me.

I'd never felt so cherished. Holden began to move, gliding in and out. It was a slow burn, the fire that built inside me. But when I looked into those dark blue eyes, I knew that fire built in him too. It was one that belonged to us alone. A unique rhythm and dance.

My hips rose up to meet him, stirring the tempo a little bit faster. I clung to Holden's shoulders as I pulled him deeper. That search for more, for all of him.

He angled his hips in the perfect way. Each time he hit that spot inside me, sparks danced. It wasn't just light in my vision, but sparks lifting from my skin. My power swirled around us.

"Holden." It was all I could say.

His forehead pressed to mine as he drove into me one more time. Those sparks shimmered and danced around us as we came apart.

"I love you, Ro. More than anything."

"Sometimes it feels like my chest will crack open with the force of it."

Holden slid out of me as he rolled us to our sides, but he didn't lose his grip on me. "I know exactly what you mean."

"It's a beautiful kind of pain, loving you all so much."

His mouth curved as his hand stroked up and down my back. "That's a good way of putting it." He pressed a kiss to the corner of my mouth. "Thank you. I needed you more than I realized."

"I'm here. Always. Whatever you need."

"It's the greatest gift I've ever been given."

My phone let out a series of dings from somewhere on the floor. The sound jarred me. No one texted me anymore. The guys tried to use texting when we were apart so that we never accidentally let people in on the fact that we could speak through our minds, but these days, we were always together.

I leaned over the side of the bed, feeling around for my device. My fingers curled around cool plastic. I lifted it and swiped my finger across the screen.

Holden leaned into me. "Who is it? They're interrupting my cuddling time."

I laughed, but the sound died on my lips as an image filled the screen. Abigail. Bound and gagged with a darkening black eye.

Unknown Number: *If you don't want your mother to die, meet me at this location in four hours. If you're a second late, she dies. You tell a soul, she dies. See you soon, daughter dearest.*

CHAPTER FORTY-FIVE

BLOOD ROARED IN MY EARS. THIS WASN'T HAPPENING. Hands framed my face. Some part of me recognized Holden.

"Breathe, Rowan. Breathe with me."

But I couldn't get my lungs to obey. Every time I tried to suck in air, it felt as if it were made of shards of ice. It sliced and clawed at my throat.

Footsteps thundered in the hallway and then Luc was there. The second his hands were on me, the worst of the panic and fear melted away. He gritted his teeth as he pulled more. He kept taking until finally I started breathing.

"What the hell happened?" Vaughn barked.

Holden motioned to the bed. "Look at her fucking phone."

Vaughn grabbed it from the mattress and let out a series of curses.

"What?" Keene asked, moving to see.

"Holden, can you get me a robe? She's shaking," Luc said.

"Of course."

I couldn't find it in me to care that Holden and I were naked

It wasn't like the guys hadn't seen it before. Holden tossed a robe to Anson, who moved to wrap it around my shoulders. He eased the fabric over my body with such tenderness, it made my nose sting.

I forced my arms to move, sliding into the sleeves, but my muscles felt cramped and rigid. "I'm okay." I looked around the room as Luc kept hold of my leg, still pulling some of the worst of the emotions. At the same time, he let that warmth that was only his trickle through our bond, comforting me.

The guys wore a mixture of expressions, from pissed the hell off to worried. My heart clenched. "We have to help her."

I struggled to my feet, searching for the bag of clothes Cass had brought over here for me from the house. "I have to get ready. He wants me to meet him someplace that's a few hours from here."

I was sure Kaleb hoped that the more distance I had from my mates, the weaker I'd be. But he was wrong. He'd gone too far. And now my rage would fuel me even when my bond wasn't close by.

"Are you out of your damn mind?" Vaughn snarled. "He baits you and you want to just walk into his trap?"

I whirled on Vaughn. "What would you have me do? He has her. The woman who gave up everything for me. If I don't try to save her, I'd never be able to live with myself."

"What good does trying to help do if you end up dead?" he pushed.

Luc released his hold on me and held up two hands. "Enough. None of this is helping. We need to think this through."

"We don't have time." I pulled clean clothes from my bag and began pulling them on.

"He's right," Keene said. "I plugged in the address. It's a trail-head in the middle of nowhere, but it'll only take two and a half hours to get there. We have time to plan."

Anson gaped at Keene. "You want her to meet him?"

He grimaced. "She has to. But she's not going alone."

I tugged my shirt over my head. "You can't. You read that text. I have to go alone."

"He won't know we're there. I've been working on some new shielding techniques. I can disguise our scents until we are on top of them."

Turning to Keene, I shook my head. "He could have some-one watching the roads. It's too risky." My best course of action was to go alone and strike as soon as Kaleb came into view. I was strong enough now. Even if the guys weren't physically with me, I carried them inside me. Our bond was giving me everything I'd never known I needed.

Holden's jaw hardened. "You aren't walking into that alone." I opened my mouth to argue, but he held up a hand. "We can take hidden access roads out the back of the pack territory. My father had them created for emergencies. Only he and I know about them."

I nibbled on the corner of my lip. "You'll stay out of sight?"

"Until you need us."

Pain lit along my sternum. "What if they outnumber us?"

"They will." Ivan's voice cut through the room as he stepped inside. "Kaleb will have more backup than you could imagine."

That pain intensified. I couldn't have my bond walk into a slaughter with me.

"Do you trust me to help?" Ivan asked.

Vaughn glared at the older man. "What are you suggesting?"

"Take as many wolves as you can afford to with you. I will put in a call to my enforcers and a few other contacts I have."

"What if one of those people decides to tip Kaleb off?" I asked. "It's clear he has sources everywhere."

Ivan shook his head. "I will only reach out to my most trusted people. I swear that to you."

I looked around the room. There were no good options here. No matter what we chose, there was the chance for devastation. But whatever we decided, we needed to make that decision together.

I opened my mind link to my bond. *What do you think?*

Luc was the first to speak. *I don't feel any deception with Ivan. It's a risk, but I think it gives us the best fighting chance.*

Vaughn growled. *I hate relying on outsiders, but strategically, Luc's right. We need more shifters on our side.*

I've been looking at the map, and I think I know where they'll hide their backup, Keene said. *I can come up with a plan that gives us the best access points for a counterattack.*

My stomach roiled at the word *attack*.

Anson shot us all a cheeky grin. *Let's fuck up some traitors and assholes.*

I looked at Holden. There was so much strain around his eyes. *This isn't just on you, Holden. It's all of us.*

He nodded. *We go with everything we have.*

CHAPTER FORTY-SIX

MY HANDS TIGHTENED AROUND THE WHEEL OF THE SUV as I made a turn on the mountain road. Anson had insisted I take the Range Rover, and as gravel turned to snow, I was glad for it. But it wasn't only the vehicle's safety I was thankful for, it was how it made me feel close to the guys.

Their scents clung to the leather and so did the memories we'd created in the space. I thought back to the first time I'd been inside, when Anson, Keene, and I had driven back to Anson's house to study. A smile curved my lips as I thought about how clueless I'd been. If you'd told me then that I could turn into a wolf or had special gifts, I would've told you that you were crazy.

Now I couldn't imagine my life without those things. Couldn't imagine my life without my mates most of all. They each gave me something so precious and unique. My chest burned as I imagined them traveling over roads opposite mine. It seemed so wrong, this separation. Yet I knew it was what we had to do.

Luc's voice broke into my mind. *You doing okay?* I felt pain

I smiled into the darkness ahead. *Your gift is getting stronger if you can feel that when we're this far away.*

He let out a soft growl. *Answer the question, Rowan.*

You're channeling some of Vaughn's bossiness.

A soft chuffing laugh sounded in my head. *Sometimes he knows the right tactics to use.*

I shook my head as if Luc could see me. *I'm okay. Just missing you all. It feels wrong to be apart like this. Especially when we're facing what's ahead.*

Luc was quiet for a moment. *None of us like it either. I still think Keene should have hidden in the Rover.*

You know they'll search it. Even if they don't scent any other shifters.

Luc let out a huff. *I don't like you being alone.*

I don't like it when any of us are alone.

A hum of energy bloomed beneath my skin.

Can you feel that? Luc asked.

My breath caught in my throat. *How?*

It was the same warmth that I had only felt when Luc was touching me. It spread through my muscle and sinew, taking root.

I've been working on projecting my gift across distances. I wasn't sure it would work this far, but our connection is unlike any other.

Tears pricked the corners of my eyes. *You're with me.*

Always, Rowan. No matter how far apart we are. No matter what stands between us. I am with you.

Luc, if you make me cry going into a battle, I'm going be really freaking pissed.

He chuckled. *Fair enough. Focus on the road. Tell us when you've arrived.*

I will. I'm close now.

Luc was quiet again for a moment. *Be safe.*

I will. I am.

Love you, Ro.

Love you too. Tell the rest of the guys too.

Will do.

His voice slipped from my mind. I should've felt cold, but the echo of Luc's energetic caress still hummed below my skin. I wasn't alone. I never would be again.

That knowledge was the most precious gift I'd ever received. I would never take it for granted. It was one of the benefits of having lost so much, of having been hurt so deeply. I knew how rare it was to receive such boundless love from five incredible guys.

That knowledge only amplified the warmth that Luc had planted. And with it, I felt them all with me.

The snow picked up as the SUV climbed higher into the mountains. I knew I was moving in the direction of Kaleb's Idaho hideout. But my destination was still within Washington state lines.

My gaze caught on a flicker of light in the distance. *I see something. I think I'm almost there.*

I sent the message to all of my mates, but it was Holden who answered. *We're in position. Keep your mind open. We should be able to read what's happening.*

And I have eyes on you, Keene said.

How?

His chuckle filled my mind. *I'm excellent at climbing trees.*

My gaze flicked to the tall pines on the mountain. They would give him the perfect vantage point. *Be careful. You could break your neck if you fall.*

I'll be careful. Promise.

Focus, Ro, Vaughn ordered. *They could attack the moment you're out of the car.*

Anson let out a growl. *Don't fill her head with that shit.*

I'm good. Focused and ready. I could feel that golden pool of energy swirling within me. I brought it to just below the surface of my skin. As soon as I had my moment, I would strike.

I pulled the SUV into a makeshift spot at the trailhead. My vision picked up three shifters in front of my vehicle. *I'm here.*

Stay open, Holden reminded me.

I sent a silent agreement. Remaining open to my bond was as easy as breathing now. I switched off the engine and slid out of the SUV. I pulled my coat around me. Even with my shifter heat, the bitter cold had a chilling effect.

A hulking figure stepped forward, flanked by two other shifters. His face was an impassive mask. "Empty your pockets."

I glared at him but did as instructed. One by one I turned the pockets of my coat inside out. Then the pockets of my jeans.

He turned to the female shifter to his right. "Search the vehicle." His gaze flicked back to me. "Don't even think of trying any of your energy tricks on me. Sal is a shield and we have others hidden in the trees."

I fought the urge to swallow. I hadn't considered the use of multiple shields at once. It wasn't something I'd ever practiced with.

Luc's voice filled my head. *It's okay. You're stronger than you could ever imagine. And we're with you.*

Ivan's here too, Holden said. *He brought his enforcers and says more reinforcements may be on the way.*

"Cat got your tongue?" the behemoth of a man asked.

I shrugged. "Why waste words when you aren't the person pulling the strings?"

Ro, watch out!

Keene yelled in my head, but it was too late. A hand latched around my throat from behind. Claws puncturing the sides of my neck.

"Did you miss me, daughter dearest?"

CHAPTER FORTY-SEVEN

I STRUGGLED TO BREATHE AS GROWLS FILLED MY HEAD.

"Is her vehicle clear?" Kaleb asked the female shifter.

"Yes, Alpha."

"And the roads to the mountain?"

"No one followed her, Alpha," the behemoth answered.

Kaleb's claws retracted and he gave me a hard shove, sending me colliding with the vehicle. His grin was all teeth. "You actually came here alone? I thought my daughter had more sense than that."

I glared at him. "You wanted me to bring my mates and my pack so that you could slaughter them, you mean?"

He chuckled, but there was no warmth in the sound. "Maybe she has more sense than I thought."

Kaleb must have given a silent command because shifters began emerging from the forest. Some were in wolf form, others human. I did a double take as my gaze caught on two familiar faces. Coby and Jasmine. Jaz sneered at me, glee in her expression as she tracked the blood trailing down my neck. Coby simply looked tired. Beaten down. She'd been sucked into a game she'd wanted no part of.

I scanned the area. There were dozens and dozens of shifters. I struggled to keep my heartbeat even. Timing. It was everything. If I attempted a strike against Kaleb now, it would only end in my death. Even if I succeeded in taking him down, his followers would converge on me.

Focusing on keeping my breathing even, I turned back to Kaleb. "Where's Abigail?"

"So willing to lay down your life for a woman who abandoned you?"

My lip curled as I let out a low growl. "She gave up everything for me. The least I can do is the same for her."

A whimper sounded from somewhere in the crowd. A second later, Abigail was being shoved towards our little gathering. The side of her face was black and blue. Her lip was cut. In that moment, I vowed to repay Kaleb for each and every injury.

"Rowan, no." Her voice broke on my name.

I hurried forward, catching her before she fell. I pushed the keys to the SUV into her hand. "Drive back to pack territory. They'll be waiting for you. Directions are plugged into the GPS."

"N-n-no. I won't leave you." Her gaze flicked to Kaleb, so much fear in her eyes. But still she was vowing not to abandon me. It meant more than I could ever say.

"I'll be okay. I promise."

Kaleb scoffed in the background.

I pressed the keys more firmly into her palm. "Go."

Abigail must've read something in my expression because she nodded slowly. I helped her into the vehicle and waited for it to start up. I watched as she slowly navigated down the hill.

Kaleb began a slow clap. "That really was touching. Something right out of the Hallmark Channel."

I gritted my teeth, turning back to him. "I'm here. What do you want?"

His eyes glinted under the moon. "There are two choices. Sever your bond or die."

Even knowing the ultimatum was coming, my pulse still spiked. "What about a third choice?"

Kaleb arched a brow. "And what did you have in mind?"

"Your death."

He let out a bellowing laugh. "And just how are you going to make that happen?"

Now! I sent the command to everyone in my pack.

In a flash, shifters descended in wolf and human form. More than I could count with how quickly they moved. Shifters from the Ridgewood pack and far more that I didn't recognize. I caught sight of Cass' bond working in tandem to dispatch a group of enforcers. Then Vaughn as he leveled shifter after shifter, crumpling them to the ground as he used his pain gift.

Anson and Luc bounded into the fray in wolf form. They worked together in perfect synchronicity. Holden stood with Keene, his gaze flicking around the battle, working to freeze our opponents whenever our wolves needed an upper hand.

Kaleb let out a snarl as wolves charged in his direction, lifting his hands to the sky. Lightning cracked and thunder rolled. I knew I needed to move now. I thrust my hands forward, sending my energy flying, but just as I released it, a wolf launched into my side.

I recognized the dark gray wolf's scent as Jasmine's, but not before her teeth sank into my side. I let out a howl of pain. My energy flew of its own volition, sinking into her fur. Her body shook and spasmed, forcing her to release me.

I scrambled to my feet, taking up a fighting position as a wolf with a blend of gold and silver fur charged towards us. Cass took up a position next to me as Jaz snarled.

Let's finish this bitch, Cass said through my mind.

It's past time. My side throbbed but none of that dulled the energy pulsing through my palms.

I struck out, but Jaz darted around the blast of light, taking a chunk out of Cass' leg. I snarled, the rage at Jaz hurting my friend only fueling me on.

Jaz feigned as if she was heading for me, but I knew she was trying to take Cass out and I was ready. I let a pulse of power fly. Jaz's eyes widened as she caught sight of it heading in her direction, but it was too late for her to change course. The blast struck her right in the chest. I knew it was fatal before Jaz even hit the ground.

The weight of her death sat heavy on my soul, but she'd given us no other choice. Cass pushed into my side. *It needed to happen.*

I knew she was right. But a life, no matter how dark it had turned, had still been lost today.

A howl split the air and everything in me froze. Because I knew that sound almost at well as my own. Luc.

CHAPTER FORTY-EIGHT

A DARK BROWN WOLF HAD SUNK HIS JAWS INTO LUC'S neck and showed no signs of stopping. Anson was close, but he was fighting off two wolves of his own. I didn't think, I simply let my energy fly. I didn't force it, didn't give it an order, I infused it with intention. To protect. To shield. To defend.

The golden light streaked through the air, splitting into three streams. Those three bolts of energy were like heat-seeking missiles. They landed with epic force, detonating in their targets. The wolves were there one second and gone the next. Then I was running.

I sank to my knees next to Luc. His chest rose and fell in rapid succession. My hands sank into his fur as my eyes closed. I pulled on that stream of golden energy, funneling it into him. *Come on, Luc.*

His body shuddered and I shoved more at him, pushing and pushing until I could feel the flesh knitting back together. *Enough. I'm okay.*

The sound of Luc's voice in my head had tears leaking from my eyes. His tongue lashed out and wiped them away.

Guys, Anson warned.

My eyes flew open to see Kaleb prowling towards us, hands raising and flanked by six enforcers. A lightning bolt hurtled in our direction. I threw up a hand, deflecting it with an energy blast of my own.

Kaleb's eyes narrowed on me. "You aren't strong enough to take me on. Surrender and I'll let your mates go free."

Anson let out a low growl, his teeth bared.

I climbed to my feet just as Holden, Keene, and Vaughn surrounded us.

My reserves were low. Too low to pierce any shielding around Kaleb. I needed time. The one thing I didn't have.

Anson pressed into my side. At the contact, a little more of my power was restored. Hope flickered.

I need you.

It was all I needed to say. Seconds later, they were all touching me. Only this time, they weren't depleting themselves to feed me. It was as if all my gift needed was to know that they were there. That we were fighting to protect our bond. My wolf howled in my head.

"Release her," Kaleb commanded.

Vaughn grinned, baring his teeth. "That'll never happen and you know it."

"Then I'll end you." He shot out another bolt of lightning but it bounced harmlessly off the shield Keene had created.

Kaleb's face reddened to a shade not found in nature. "End them all!"

Panic lit through me as the shifters around us fought with a renewed fervor. It was almost as if something otherworldly had taken over their forms.

Kaleb's mouth pulled into a sneer. "Didn't I tell you? I have a little help."

He glanced in the direction of the woods. That same man I'd seen in the jail cell was there. The warlock.

"Dark magic," Holden hissed.

Kaleb smirked at him. "True dominants do whatever it takes to win. It's what you and your father never understood."

Holden's eyes flashed. "That isn't dominance. It's the destruction of your soul."

Kaleb chuckled.

I couldn't hear whatever words he spoke next. I was too overcome by the shifters fighting desperately around us. For survival, for what was right. I couldn't let them die. Not in a battle I'd brought them into.

Energy swirled within me. It twisted into a funnel, almost like a tornado. I'd never felt anything like it before and panic started to set in. My wolf spoke to me then. Her voice clear as day. *Trust me. Trust us.*

I'd battled so much with my gift, but every time I'd taken the step to trust it, that gift had defended me. It had been protecting me at every step. I had to let it free.

I sent one single message to my bond. *Love you with all I am.*

I released the power. That energy within me flew from my body. These were no simple sparks. This was a wave of sheer force. And it seemed to go on forever.

Kaleb's eyes widened as the wall of raw power charged towards him. It ate through the shield around him as if it were merely air. The enforcers surrounding him crumpled to the ground, but that wasn't enough for my gift when it came to Kaleb.

The bands of energy circled him. One lashed at his cheek and lip, recreating the wounds he had given Abigail. Another lashed at his neck, giving the same puncture wounds he'd assaulted me with. Then it closed off his airway altogether.

I could feel the darkness in him as my power connected with his form. It was made of a decay that couldn't be undone. He'd given too much of his soul in the quest for rule. For more. There was only one choice. To end him.

My gift knew it too. The bands tightened, and in one swift move, Kaleb's neck snapped. As he fell to the ground, my energy pulsed out again. It swept over the field.

I watched in awe as it consumed the shifters around us. With each creature it met, I got another piece of the puzzle. It was fueled by my entire bond, made up of all of us.

It used Luc's empathy to read the intentions of each shifter it met, to mete out justice or to protect. It used Keene's shield to protect those with pure hearts. Holden's ability to freeze those with bad intent. Anson's strength and Vaughn's pain to bring those who wished to do evil to their knees.

The wave of power coursed over the mountainside. The warlock's eyes widened and he started to run. But he was no match for my bond. Our energy engulfed him as he screamed.

As soon as he was brought to his knees, the power snapped back to me with a force that had me rocking sideways. And then everything went black.

CHAPTER FORTY-NINE

I WAS AWASH IN SENSATION. THE SOUNDS OF MUTED VOICES. The feel of hands stroking my skin and hair. I let out a soft moan.

The hands touching me stilled.

"Rowan?" It was Holden's voice that broke through my haze.

I blinked a few times. The light in the room was muted by drawn curtains, but it still took time for my vision to adjust.

Keene's thumbs stroked over my cheeks. "How do you feel?"

I started to speak, but my words came out as a croak.

"Here." Anson lifted my head as Luc brought a straw to my lips.

I pulled in deep gulps of water. It was heaven on a throat that was as dry as the desert. "Hi."

My voice still resembled a toad's, but at least my word was decipherable. "How long was I out?"

Vaughn glared at me as if going unconscious had been my choice. "Two days."

My eyes widened as memories flew across my mind. The battle. Kaleb. My power surge.

I bolted upright, my vision blurring. "Our pack. Is everyone okay? Abigail? Mason? Ivan?"

Luc's hands gripped my shoulders, easing me back onto the pillows. "Slow down. Everyone's okay."

My gaze narrowed on him.

He held up a hand. "There were some injuries, but Ivan and Cinna brought in their healers to help. And Ivan healed some of the shifters himself."

My brows lifted. "Cinna?"

Amusement played on Holden's lips. "Apparently that was one of the calls Ivan made. He told her if she wanted to know the truth to show up at the mountain. She couldn't resist the challenge."

"And when she saw what Kaleb was doing, she and her enforcers fought along with us," Keene said.

"Never thought I'd be thankful for her," I muttered.

"Me neither," Anson echoed.

I lifted my gaze to Holden. "Your dad?"

The smile that lit his face put me at ease. He squeezed my leg. "He's home. Thanks to Ivan's guards, the worst abuse he got was on his way to the prison. I'm trying to get him to take it easy, but of course, he refuses."

Keene tucked a strand of hair behind my ear. "It's good he feels up to a challenge because Abigail has been pestering him to let her see you since we brought you back."

"She's okay?"

Keene nodded. "Jumpy, but physically, she's fine. Her mind will ease with time."

"Especially knowing all of Kaleb's enforcers and those who fought with him are imprisoned now," Anson added.

My jaw hardened. "What happens to them?"

"A trial," Holden explained. "They will be tried as a group as soon as new members of the Quad have been chosen."

"Members?"

Luc grinned. "Gregor hightailed it to somewhere in Europe, but apparently, he left before he paid the rogues that he and Kaleb hired to kidnap those girls. Rogues don't take kindly to those who don't pay their debts."

"Pretty sure they'll be finding pieces of him all over Russia for the next fifty years," Keene muttered.

I couldn't find it in me to be sorry about that. "They found the girls?"

Holden nodded. "They're safe with family in other packs now."

Relief swamped me, but on its heels, confusion rose. "I still don't understand why Gregor was helping Kaleb."

The guys shared a look, but it was Keene who spoke. "One of his enforcers came forward to Ivan and Cinna. Apparently, Gregor was helping Kaleb get the pieces in place to return to a monarchy, but he planned for an unfortunate accident to take him out at the last minute."

"So he could become king," I surmised.

"Instead, he's fleshy confetti thanks to a bunch of rogues," Anson said with a little too much glee.

I scrunched up my nose. "Gross."

Keene smacked Anson on the back of the head. "Let's not make her nauseated, okay?"

Vaughn wove his fingers through mine. "How do you feel?"

I did a mental inventory. "Stiff, a little sore, but fine."

Doubt filled Vaughn's expression, but under that, I saw worry and fear. I sat up, leaning towards him. I lifted my hands to his face. "Hey, I'm fine. I promise."

"You maxed yourself out," he growled.

"And then you replenished me. It's how this works."

He scowled. "You're never doing that again. It was too much power for one person to wield."

"It wasn't one person. It was six. The only way that was possible was through all of us." My thumbs stroked over his stubbled cheeks. "Balance. But I need to get used to being a vessel for it all."

"I don't like it—"

I cut him off with a kiss. If Vaughn wouldn't believe my words, maybe he would believe my actions. My tongue stroked his, silently reassuring him that I was okay.

He growled into my mouth and then tore his lips away. "You need to rest."

My brow quirked. "Do I?"

Anson chuckled. "I like where your mind is at."

Luc's lips skimmed my shoulder. "Let us take care of you."

"I don't need—"

Keene stole my words with his lips. And then I was lost in his kiss. As he lowered me back to the bed, the covers were tugged free. Fingers hooked in my sleep shorts and pulled them down. Cool air met my overheated flesh as my tank top was sliced in half with claws.

I couldn't find it in me to argue about it being my favorite. Not when Anson latched on to one nipple and Holden the other. Anson nipped at the peak and then laved the sting with that incredible tongue.

Two fingers slid inside me. Vaughn stroking in long, languid motions. Luc's finger circled my clit. He used that magical knowledge of sensation, his psychic map of my body to drive me higher. He made tighter and tighter circles but never quite got to exactly where I wanted him.

My hips rose up, seeking that final piece of contact. Luc chuckled. "Impatient?"

I moaned into Keene's mouth. He broke away from the kiss. "She needs more."

A third finger slid inside me. Vaughn curled those fingers and I whimpered.

"Come on, Luc. I want to watch her come," Keene said.

Holden sucked my nipple deep, and I let out another strangled sound.

Luc took pity on me then. His head dipped and his tongue flicked across my clit. Once, twice, three times. Each swipe of his tongue made those sparks dance around us. Then he closed his lips over that bundle of nerves.

The riot of sensations he created with his mouth warred with those the rest of my guys wrung out of my body. I didn't know where one of us ended and the others began. All I knew was the safety and peace that was being lost in their arms. I never wanted anything else.

CHAPTER FIFTY

WE LAY IN A TANGLE OF LIMBS. HANDS STROKED MY bare skin as energy still hummed around us. "I love you," I said softly. "I never thought I could be as happy or feel as safe as when I'm with you, all of us together."

Anson nuzzled my neck. "I wasn't sure how it was possible for us to work as a whole. But it does. It makes this weird sort of perfection."

Keene hit him with a pillow. "Who are you calling weird?"

Luc chuckled and kissed my hip. "We love you too."

"So damn much," Holden echoed.

"So damn much that I don't even mind the rest of these assholes that much," Vaughn piped in.

I couldn't hold in my laughter.

A polite knock sounded in all of our minds. Mason's voice filled the mental space. *I know you're probably resting, but Ivan and Cinna are here to see Rowan.*

You have got to be kidding me, Anson griped.

The last thing I wanted to do was leave this bed, but they'd both fought by our sides. The least I could do was have a conversation. *I'll come down.*

Give us thirty minutes, Holden added. He smiled at me. "They can wait while you shower."

"While we *all* shower," Anson quipped.

And because of that, it was more like an hour before we made it to the lodge.

Ivan gave me a gentle smile as I lowered myself to the couch. He leaned forward in his seat. "How are you feeling?"

"Good. Relieved."

"I'm sure."

"How are you? You weren't hurt, were you?"

He shook his head. "You've got to be quick to mess with these old bones."

Cinna rolled her eyes. "He's old because he's outlived all his enemies by killing them off."

Ivan chuckled. "Is that such a bad thing?"

"I said it as a compliment," Cinna argued.

I stifled a laugh and lifted my gaze to Cinna's. "Thank you for helping us."

Her lips pursed. "I don't like being wrong."

Ivan snorted. "No kidding."

She shot him a withering glare. "So it pains me to say that I was. I should've listened to you. I'm embarrassed at how I believed Gregor and Kaleb's lies."

"When you realized the truth, you stood up for it. That's what matters."

Cinna and Ivan shared a look, then Ivan's gaze circled the

room, sweeping over the guys, me, and finally landing on Mason. "All charges against you have been expunged."

Mason dipped his head. "Thank you."

"I'm sorry it was ever on your record in the first place," Cinna said.

"I've restored his Alpha status," Holden added. "Does that mean his seat on the council is in place again as well?"

Cinna nodded. "It is."

Ivan cleared his throat, eyes shifting to me and then back to Mason. "We're actually here to invite Mason and Rowan to compete in the Quad trials. We would be honored to have you amongst our ranks."

The room went completely still. I could feel the anxious protests from my mates. Those trials were brutal, and death was a regular occurrence.

Mason leaned back in his chair. "I'm honored you would consider me, but I'm happy here. Leading my pack, spending time with my family. Politics isn't something I'm interested in."

"Which is exactly why we need you," Ivan pushed.

He had a point there. It was the reluctant leaders that typically did the most for their people. Yet everything about this was wrong.

"Haven't you learned anything?" I asked.

While my voice was quiet, it echoed in the still space.

Cinna's shoulders straightened. "Excuse me?"

"You would put us back into the same system, knowing how broken it is?"

"Rowan," Ivan began. "We've rooted out the decay—"

"For now. But you're giving it room to grow again by allowing these barbaric traditions to continue. If you truly love your people, give them a voice. Let them elect who will lead. Give them access to the ruling body. That is what will bring us together."

Cinna's mouth snapped closed. "It's annoying when she has a perfectly good point."

Ivan chuckled. "She has a way of doing that." His expression sobered. "We need people like you to lead. People like Mason."

I glanced at Mason. He'd given me a safe space in his pack. A home. I'd learned so much from him in the short time that I'd been here. "If you bring us into a democracy, I promise you I'll put my name in the hat."

I didn't have to ask my mates what they thought of it. I could feel their pride in me, in my being asked. But more, I could feel their pride at my determination to change how things were done in our world.

I was strong enough to demand it because I knew they were with me every step of the way, no matter what we faced. Just like I would be with them, wherever their destinies took them. That bond made us stronger than anything that lay ahead, and I knew we would be happy and content, just as long as we were together.

EPILOGUE

FIVE YEARS LATER

"Okay, add a cup of the dry ingredients." I set the mixer on low as Crispin followed my instructions. Over the years, the chocolate crinkle cookies had become a staple. They marked celebrations, difficult moments, and sometimes just everyday whims. And Crispin had become my very best assistant.

Afternoons like this one were some of my favorites. All of my guys were scattered about the house while I spent some quality time with the now fourteen-year-old. He'd been quiet today, but I'd come to realize that was simply the way Crispin was when he was working up to something. I simply let him be, and eventually, he'd get there all on his own.

I motioned for him to add a bit more of the cocoa powder mixture, my rings catching on the light. There wasn't a time they didn't make me smile. My engagement ring held a setting of five stones, one for each of my mates. My jaw had nearly hit the floor when they'd given it to me on my twentieth birthday.

Humans thought I was too young. There'd been whispers around town about me being pregnant. I'd just rolled my eyes and enjoyed my happy. No small-minded people were going to ruin it for me.

The day we'd all pledged our lives to one another on the cliffs behind our house had been the best of my life. My adoptive parents had never reentered my life, but that was all right. They'd given me care for a time, and I'd always be thankful for that. Instead, I was surrounded by those who would walk with me forever.

The woman I now felt comfortable calling Mom helped me every step of the way. From picking out a dress to choosing the perfect flowers. When I'd asked Mason to walk me down the aisle, he'd shed a few tears and told me it would be his honor. Cass had stood at my side as I promised my mates eternity and beyond. And it was Ivan who had bound us together.

Even though we already knew forever had been written in the stars, there was something about saying it out loud that had been another level of intimacy.

"I asked Heather to homecoming."

My hand jerked on the mixer at Crispin's words. I shut it off and turned towards him. "That's a big move."

Crispin winced. "I know she's human, but I *really* like her, Ro."

Oh, teenage hormones. I knew how those worked. "If your heart's telling you to go in that direction, then you should listen to it."

Others in our pack would say it was foolish, that humans and shifters shouldn't mix. But I would never shut down Crispin that way. I wrapped an arm around his shoulders, pulling him in for a hug. "Don't listen to anyone else. You do what you think is right."

He grinned. "Will you help me pick out a suit?"

My nose stung and my eyes watered. "You couldn't keep me away."

My mom bustled into the kitchen. "We gotta get going, C. You have practice in thirty minutes." She sent me a knowing look. "These first dances are a killer."

I grinned even if there were tears in my eyes. Abigail had taken Crispin in on a permanent basis. It had been exactly what she'd needed to come back to life. And if there was one thing I knew, it was that no one loved harder than she did.

I gave Crispin one last squeeze and released him. "We'll go after school tomorrow. Ask Heather what color dress she's wearing."

He scrunched up his nose. "Why?"

I ruffled his hair. "Because we'll match your tie to her dress, and she'll think you are the most swoon-worthy date she's ever had."

Crispin's eyes brightened at that. "I'll text her tonight."

My mom waved, following after Crispin. I grabbed a tissue from the box by the phone, dabbing at my eyes. Arms came around my waist as Vaughn nuzzled my neck. "What's with the tears?"

"He's growing up so fast."

Vaughn chuckled against my skin.

I smacked his arm. "Don't laugh at me."

"I love your tender heart."

"I love yours too."

And Vaughn had let us see more and more of it as time had gone on.

He pressed a kiss to my shoulder as the timer went off. "That what I think it is?"

I opened the oven and pulled out the first batch of crinkle cookies. "Crispin and I decided we should make dough for this weekend too."

"I knew I liked that kid."

"Will you grab the rest of the guys?"

Instead of going to find them, Vaughn simply opened our mental channel. *Get your asses down here unless you want me to eat all the cookies.*

I made a face. "That's not what I meant."

"If I made the rounds, half of these would be gone by the time I made it back." He gave my shoulder a playful nip. "You know I don't mess around with your cookies."

I snorted as footsteps thundered on the stairs. No matter how old we were, cookies still had the guys reverting to juvenile status and I hoped that never changed.

Keene grunted as Anson elbowed him in the gut and then dove towards the cooling rack. I smacked Anson's hand with my spatula.

"Ow," he said, shaking it out.

"They're too hot. You'll burn your mouth and then you'll be begging me to heal you so you can eat more cookies."

He dipped his head for a kiss. "Is that really so bad?"

I shook my head. "It's a waste."

Luc moved in behind me, massaging my shoulders. "How was your Quad meeting?"

"Good, but long. We were dividing up this year's mentorship recipients."

His thumbs dug deeper into my muscles. "You love that."

I grinned. I did love it. The program had been my brainchild, a way to reach all the young people in the packs and give them a chance to learn more about the leadership opportunities they could have in the future. "I love it, but it's exhausting."

Holden moved in, ghosting a thumb over the dark circles under my eyes. "You should go to bed early tonight. That stomach bug took it out of you. We can postpone the event this weekend—"

"Don't you dare." I pointed my spatula at him. "Becoming Alpha is a huge honor, we aren't postponing that for a second."

"I love it when she gets bossy like that," Keene quipped.

Holden chuckled and kissed my temple. "Okay, fine. This weekend it is. But you have to rest between now and then."

"I can do that." Nerves bubbled up in my stomach and Luc gave me a funny look.

"What's wrong?"

I set the spatula on the counter. Hiding this from my bond had been exhausting, but I'd wanted to be one hundred percent sure and things had been so busy lately. There'd barely been time with all six of us together and alone.

"Nothing's wrong. I just—I have some news."

Five pairs of eyes shifted to me.

It had been my mother who had shown me the shielding magic required to disguise my scent. It was the same magic she'd used to disguise her own all those years ago. I let the shield drop and waited.

Nostrils flared and eyes widened.

"Rowan," Holden said, his voice thick with emotion.

"Good surprise? It's not stealing your thunder, is it?"

He moved in, his hand going to my belly. "A pup with you? Nothing could be better."

Luc's hand joined his on my stomach. "How long?"

"Just a couple of weeks."

Keene's eye flared as he closed the distance. "This is why you weren't feeling well?"

I nodded. "That nausea was awful."

Vaughn moved in a flash, scooping me up in his arms. "You shouldn't be on your feet. You need to rest." He carried me into the living room, setting me on the couch so gently, you would've thought I was made of glass.

"I'm not going to break."

He let out a soft growl and touched his forehead to mine. "Precious cargo all the way around."

My gaze swept the room. "So you're all happy?" They looked at me like I was crazy for even asking the question. "We weren't trying."

Keene grinned. "We weren't not trying either."

Anson sank to his knees next to the couch, lifting my shirt and palming my still-flat belly. "Ro." Tears filled his eyes. "How could we not be happy? You've given us all a family."

My own tears spilled then. Because that was the greatest gift of all.

THE END

ACKNOWLEDGMENTS

My biggest thank you has to go to YOU! Yes, you. I'm incredibly grateful that you have continued on Rowan's journey with me. This magical world has been exactly what I needed when there has been so much hardship in our real world. I hope Rowan and her guys have been an escape for you as well. Thank you for supporting me along the way!

So many people have walked alongside me in the creation of this book. A huge thank you to my editorial team, proofers, and cover designers. To the couple of early readers of this series who gave me such enthusiastic encouragement. And to my amazing writer friends who have cheered me on every step of the way.

ALSO BY TESSA HALE

The Shifting Fate Series
Spark of Fate
Mark of Stars
Bond of Destiny

For a full list of up-to-date Tessa Hale titles please visit
www.tessahale.com.

CONNECT WITH TESSA

You can find Tessa at various places on the internet. These are her favorites…

Website
www.tessahale.com

Newsletter
www.tessahale.com/newsletter

Facebook Page
https://bit.ly/TessaHaleFB

Facebook Reader Group
https://bit.ly/TessaHaleBookHangout

Instagram
www.instagram.com/tessahalewrites

Goodreads
https://bit.ly/TessaHaleGR

BookBub
www.bookbub.com/authors/tessa-hale

Amazon
https://bit.ly/TessaHaleAmazon

ABOUT TESSA HALE

Author of love stories with magic, usually with more than one love interest. Constant daydreamer.

Printed in Great Britain
by Amazon

11505947R00153